EVIL
AT
THE
ROOT

Also by Bill Crider

EVIL

AT

THE

ROOT

BILL CRIDER

ST. MARTIN'S PRESS NEW YORK

Design by Robert Bull Design

Library of Congress Cataloging-in-Publication Data

Crider, Bill,
        Evil at the root / Bill Crider.
                p.   cm.
        "A Thomas Dunne book"
        ISBN 0–312–04314–7
        I. Title.
        PS3553.R497E95   1990
        813'.54—dc20   89–78097

First Edition
10 9 8 7 6 5 4 3 2 1

To Angela and Allen

CHAPTER
ONE

It was a brisk morning—48 degrees on the jailhouse thermometer—and Sheriff Dan Rhodes had all the windows rolled up on the county car. It didn't matter, though. He could still hear the little man yelling at him as he parked in the lot of the Sunny Dale Nursing Home.

"Ah ain't got no teef! Ah ain't got no teef!"

The man had on a Western-style straw hat, not exactly appropriate for the weather; a white Western shirt that was buttoned at the collar and seemed to have been made for a neck about two sizes larger than the one that was in it; very clean blue jeans, newly pressed with a sharp crease down the front; and black cowboy boots. Over the white shirt he wore a puffy insulated ski jacket, unzipped. It was electric blue with a bright red band circling the chest. His face was red and scraped from his morning shave, and he was quivering with anger.

"Ah ain't got no teef!" he yelled. "Ah ain't got no teef!" His voice was thin and high, but strong.

Rhodes walked up to the porch. The little man came up to about his shoulders and probably didn't weigh more than ninety pounds. His eyes were red and rheumy.

1

The porch was lined with chairs, but the man wasn't sitting in one. He was standing in the sun to keep warm, though Rhodes suspected that anger was keeping his blood pretty hot.

"I'm the sheriff," Rhodes said, indicating the badge case on his belt. "What's this about your teeth?"

"Ah ain't got no teef!" the man yelled.

Rhodes resisted the urge to put his hands over his ears.

The man stopped yelling and pointed to his mouth. There were no teeth in there, that was for sure. It was just a smooth-rimmed black hole surrounded by chapped lips.

"I'd better check with Mr. Patterson," Rhodes told the little man. He opened one of the big glass doors and started inside.

"Ah ain't got no teef!" the man yelled behind him.

Rhodes let the door swing shut. He was in the lobby now, the sun coming in through all the glass and making the somewhat worn furniture look as cheerful as possible. There were no visitors sitting there yet, but it was still early in the day.

Rhodes was not overly fond of nursing homes, no matter how much sunshine there was in the lobby. He didn't like their peculiar odor; he didn't like the rails on the walls, there to help the people walk without falling down; and he especially didn't like to think that he was not getting any younger himself, though that was certainly the case. Besides, they were always too hot in the winter, in deference to what Texans considered the well-known fact that people's blood thinned out as they got older, a condition that caused them to suffer more from the cold than younger folks.

Rhodes had visited Sunny Dale before in the course of his job, when some of the residents had rioted to protest certain rules they thought were unfair. He had later attended the marriage ceremony performed for two of those residents, Mr. Stuart and Mrs. White, and he had visited them several times since then.

Familiarity had not endeared the place to him, though he knew that it was well-run and that the residents were well cared for. He still hoped that he would never wind up there.

He walked to the reception desk. Earlene, whose last name Rhodes had never learned and who shared reception duties with a black woman named Linda, sat in a chair behind the desk. She was reading a tattered, dog-eared copy of *Cosmopolitan* that she had probably picked up from the visitors' area.

"Good morning, Earlene," Rhodes said.

She looked up from her magazine. "Hi, Sheriff." She giggled. "That's a joke. Get it? 'Hi, Sheriff'? It's like High Sheriff."

Just in case he still didn't get it, she spelled it out. "You know. Like H-I-G-H Sheriff?"

Rhodes tried to laugh convincingly. "Is Mr. Patterson around?" he asked.

Earlene stood up, laid her magazine down with the spine up to save her place, and leaned over the counter. "It's about Mr. Bobbit's teeth, isn't it?" she said in a conspiratorial whisper.

"I'm not sure I ought to say anything about it until I've talked to Mr. Patterson," Rhodes said.

"Hell, honey, we all know about it," Earlene said. "You'd be surprised at what-all gets stolen around here. Candy bars, money, jewelry boxes, all kinds of stuff. A toothbrush now and then, even. This is the first time for teeth, though. I tell you, these old people, they'll—"

"That's enough, Earlene," Mr. Patterson said, coming up behind her from his office. "I'll handle this."

He stuck his hand across the counter to Rhodes, and Rhodes shook it. It was soft and white, like the rest of the man. Patterson obviously didn't get out in the sun much,

3

and he was even dressed in white, right down to a pair of gum-soled white shoes. He had carefully styled blond hair that was sprayed stiff, every individual hair in its place.

"Let's go in my office," he suggested, and Rhodes went around the counter and followed him in. It was a small, cramped room, most of the space taken up by a wooden desk and a gray metal filing cabinet. The top of the desk was neatly arranged, papers in three separate piles, and Rhodes couldn't help envying Patterson's ability to keep things in their places.

Patterson went behind his desk and sat down, asking Rhodes to take the only other seat in the room, an uncomfortable wooden chair with a straight back and no cushion.

"What's this about the teeth?" Rhodes said.

Mr. Patterson touched his hair with his right hand as if to smooth it down. Rhodes figured there was so much hairspray on it that touching it would be like touching baling wire.

"Someone stole Mr. Bobbit's teeth," Mr. Patterson said.

"I gather that's Mr. Bobbit on the porch," Rhodes said, squirming a little in the chair. It didn't help. He still couldn't get comfortable.

"Yes," Mr. Patterson said. "That's him all right. A dear gentleman, most of the time."

"He seems a little upset about the teeth, though," Rhodes said.

Patterson smiled weakly. "Yes. Well, it's not him so much as his daughter. Seems to hold me personally liable, though of course I'm not." He looked sharply at Rhodes. "Am I?"

"You'd have to check with your lawyer about that," Rhodes said.

"Oh. Well, I will. Still, Miss Bobbit is very insistent that we find the teeth. And of course, it is pretty hard for Mr. Bobbit to eat without them." Patterson touched the left

4

side of his hair this time. "Not that we don't have things that he can eat perfectly well. We do, all sorts of things. But he does miss his teeth."

Rhodes nodded. "So I gathered." He was thinking about having to eat strained prunes or pureed vegetables or something equally horrible for every meal. "Can't say that I blame him."

"Naturally. That's why I called you. I hoped that you'd investigate and see what you could do."

"Couldn't he just have lost his teeth? Misplaced them?"

"We thought about that, but there's really no place for them to be, at least not in his room. We searched very carefully."

Rhodes thought about it. This kind of theft, if that was what it was, wasn't exactly the kind of thing the taxpayers wanted their sheriff to spend his time on. Still, he might be able to do something without sacrificing any time from his other duties. Patterson was a taxpayer, too.

"I'll try to help out," he said, standing up.

Patterson stood too, putting out his hand for another shake. "Thank you, Sheriff. If there's anything that I can do to assist you, please don't hesitate to ask."

"All you need to do is let me talk to a few people," Rhodes said.

"Of course. Of course. Anyone in particular?"

"I thought I'd start with Mr. Bobbit."

"Well, Mr. Bobbit . . . I mean, you met Mr. Bobbit."

"On the porch."

"Yes. Then you know . . ."

"I want to talk to him anyway."

"Of course. Of course. Go right ahead."

Mr. Bobbit was still on the porch where Rhodes had left him.

A man and a woman about Rhodes's age had gotten out

5

of their car and were trying to get through the front door, probably to visit a relative or friend.

Mr. Bobbit was yelling at them. "Ah ain't got no teef!"

The man, pudgy and red-faced, wearing a gray felt hat, was trying to maneuver around him on one side, his wife, also pudgy, on the other.

But Mr. Bobbit wasn't having any of it. They weren't going to get by him like Rhodes had. He was moving from one side of the doors to the other, yelling.

"Ah ain't got no teef!"

Rhodes went outside. He was sweating under his shirt because of the heat in the building, and the sudden chill of the air felt very good. "Mr. Bobbit?" he said.

Surprised, Mr. Bobbit spun around. The pudgy man and woman scooted past him and through the door, looking back gratefully at Rhodes. He hoped they'd remember him at the next election.

"Did someone steal your teeth?" he asked Mr. Bobbit.

The old man looked immensely pleased that someone had figured it out. "Dod-damn wight! Sum'buddy stole 'em!"

"Who did it, do you think?"

That stumped Mr. Bobbit temporarily. He quit moving around and stared at the concrete porch beneath his feet. Or maybe he was looking at the toes of his boots poking out from beneath the bottoms of the jeans.

"Mr. Bobbit?" Rhodes said.

The old man's head jerked up. "An ain't got no teef!"

Rhodes nodded. "Right. And who do you think might have taken them?"

Mr. Bobbit went into another trance, and Rhodes was about to give it all up as a bad job, when the old man spoke again.

"Mighta been 'at Dod-damn Mah-weece Kenn'dy."

"Maurice Kennedy?"

"'At's what Ah said. Dod-damn sumbitch."

6

"Does Mr. Kennedy live here?"

"Ah ain't got no teef!"

Rhodes decided that he had learned just about as much as he could from Mr. Bobbit. He left the old man to his anger, which seemed to be about all he had left, and went back inside.

He didn't stop at the desk to ask Earlene about Mr. Kennedy. He had a feeling that anything he said to her might just as well be published in the local newspaper. Instead, he walked down the hall of what had been known as Sunny Dale's "men's wing" until the riots. Now that Mr. Stuart and Mrs. White were man and wife and were being allowed to live together, there was no more separation of the sexes. No more riots, either.

Rhodes tried not to look into any of the open doors as he walked along the hallway. Though some of the elderly residents of Sunny Dale were spry and lively, the Stuarts being a case in point, others were invalids, seemingly without any spark of life or hope. They often sat in their chairs studying the floor for hours on end, or they lay in their beds staring endlessly and blankly at color television sets, their eyes as unblinking as the screens.

Once upon a time they had rolled on the lawn with collie dogs, played hide-and-seek and baseball, fallen in love, borne children, had families, worked at jobs they loved or hated. And now this. What really bothered Rhodes was that he was a lot closer to them in age than he was to a kid playing hide-and-seek.

The depression that he usually felt in the nursing home lifted a bit when he went into the Stuarts' room. They had a television set, but it was hardly ever on. They preferred to read or to play draw poker.

Mrs. Stuart liked Stephen King and was a steely-eyed opponent at the game table. Rhodes had sat in for a few hands of penny ante once and lost fifty-seven cents to her in about fifteen minutes.

Mr. Stuart read mostly mysteries, and his greatest wish was to live long enough to read every hard-boiled private-eye novel so far published in a large-print edition. He was nowhere near the poker player his wife was, and had told Rhodes on a recent visit that he was down five thousand dollars at the last accounting. Fortunately they didn't play for real money, just kept a running tab. That way, Rhodes didn't have to arrest them for running a high-stakes illegal gambling operation.

They were both well over eighty years of age and were quite frail, but their health was in general very good, and their marriage seemed to have made them even more energetic and spirited than they had been before.

They were seated at the small table in the center of their room when Rhodes entered through the open door.

He didn't say anything, just glanced at Mr. Stuart's hand—two pairs, nines and tens—and went to stand behind Mrs. Stuart. She had a pair of threes in her own hand, which she couldn't quite hold steady.

"I'll see your twenty and raise you fifty," she said in her quavery voice, shoving five red chips to the center of the table and staring into her husband's eyes.

Mr. Stuart was wearing a sport coat that looked about three sizes too big. He looked back at his wife for a second or two, then sighed and folded his hand.

"Too rich for my blood," he said. "What did you have?"

"You know better than to ask that," Mrs. Stuart said, folding her own hand and slipping it into the deck. "You have to pay to see." She pulled the small pile of chips over to her side of the table, where she had already accumulated quite a stack.

"How're you, Sheriff?" she said.

"Fine," Rhodes said. "Been at it long?"

"'Bout an hour," Mr. Stuart said. He had a tendency to talk a little louder than was really necessary. "Ivy come with you?"

Ivy Daniel was Rhodes's fiancée. They were going to be married in one week, on February 27.

"Not this time," Rhodes said. "I'm here on business."

"I bet it's about those teeth," Mr. Stuart said.

"That's right," Rhodes told him. "Does everybody in here know everything that goes on?"

"Pretty much," Mrs. Stuart said. "There's not much else to do except keep up with everybody's business."

"What about the teeth, then? You know who took them?"

Mrs. Stuart shook her head. It was a little wobbly on her thin neck. Her hair was completely white and very short.

"Not yet, we don't," she said.

"Not yet?"

"She thinks she's got a way to find out," Mr. Stuart said. "I've got a bet with her for half my losses."

"He'll lose on this, just like he does at cards," Mrs. Stuart said. "I'll just scut down the hall in my walker when they feed us today, and I'll watch to see who's enjoyin' himself the most while he eats. You can bet it'll be somebody with new teeth, somebody who hasn't been eatin' well lately."

It sounded to Rhodes like as good a way as any to find out. "It wasn't either one of you, was it?"

Mr. Stuart grinned, exposing his own choppers, of which there appeared to be about six. "Got my own teeth," he said proudly. "Don't need anybody else's."

"Me, too," his wife said, though she didn't offer to show them.

"How about Maurice Kennedy?"

Mrs. Stuart thought about it for a second or two. "Might've been. He strikes me as a sneaky type, all right. I'll pay special attention to him. But he and Mr. Bobbit are supposed to be friends from way back."

Rhodes had never met Kennedy. "I'll pay him a visit," he said.

9

"If you do that, I won't have much of a chance to win my bet," Mrs. Stuart said.

Rhodes didn't see any harm in letting the old woman have her fun. "I won't talk to him until tomorrow, then," he said. "But don't try to do anything except look. I'll tell Mr. Patterson that the case is in good hands."

"I'm still bettin' she don't find out," Mr. Stuart said. "I figure to get back around three thousand dollars out of this."

"Ha," Mrs. Stuart said. "You'll just be nine thousand in the hole, is what you'll be."

"We'll see. Let's play another hand or two. I feel lucky today. You want to sit in, Sheriff?" He was putting the cards into a mechanical shuffler that sat on the table.

"No, thanks," Rhodes said. "I've got to get back to the jail, see what's going on around the county. I'll see you two later."

"You bring Ivy next time," Mr. Stuart said.

"I'll try to do that," Rhodes assured him. He left the room and went back down the hall to Mr. Patterson's office, told him that the investigation was continuing, and went back outside.

"Ah ain't got no teef!" Mr. Bobbit announced when Rhodes came through the doors.

"I'm working on it," Rhodes told him. He went to his car and got in.

"Ah ain't got no teef!" Mr. Bobbit yelled as Rhodes drove away.

It was the last time Rhodes saw him alive.

CHAPTER
TWO

When Rhodes got back to the jail, Hack Jensen was in a state of high dudgeon, a condition Rhodes had read about but which he was pretty sure he'd never actually witnessed.

There was no doubt that he was witnessing it now.

Hack was even more outraged than Mr. Bobbit had been. If he'd been a cartoon character, smoke would have been pouring from his ears.

Lawton, the jailer, was equally upset, hopping from one foot to the other. He was short and stout, and right now he was so red-faced that Rhodes thought a heart attack might be imminent.

"What's going on here?" Rhodes said. "You two look like you're about to explode."

Hack, the dispatcher, was sitting at his table with the radio and telephone. He picked up a sheaf of papers and rattled them at Rhodes. "Upset? I guess I am! And you will be too, when you find out what's goin' on around here!"

Rhodes had a sinking feeling in the pit of his stomach. If he had to depend on Hack and Lawton to get the story told, he might not find out until the next week. Their main pleasure in life seemed to be knowing something that Rhodes didn't know and making him wait as long as possible to find it out.

He decided to give Lawton a try. "Do you know what he's talking about?"

"Do I know? Of course I know. Hell, he told me first off. It makes my blood boil, let me tell you."

"What does?" Rhodes asked.

"Them papers, that's what! I swear, I never in my life—"

"What about the papers?" Rhodes asked.

"We got 'em this mornin', right after you left for the nursin' home," Hack said, avoiding the question.

Rhodes gave it up. As always, he was going to get the story their way, and in their own good time. He went to his desk and sat down, leaning back a little in his chair.

"All right," he said when he was comfortable. "Let's have it."

"Well," Hack said, "this man came in lookin' for you."

"Had on a dark blue suit," Lawton added. "One of those with the fine little blue stripes in it, so fine you can't hardly see 'em."

" 'Course we knew he was a lawyer right off," Hack said. "Anybody dresses like that must be either a lawyer or a banker, and we don't get a whole lot of bankers in the jail."

"Could've been a bondsman," Lawton put in. "Couple of them wear suits."

"Wasn't no bondsman, either," Hack said.

"Who was it?" Rhodes asked, hating himself for trying to get to the point. He knew it wouldn't do any good.

"Now that was the interestin' part," Lawton said. "We didn't know who he was, and I guess we know about ever' lawyer in Blacklin County, don't we, Hack?"

"You got that right. They've all been in here at one time or another, and if he was a local, we'd know him. But like Lawton said, we didn't know him, which meant he wasn't from around here."

"Turns out he's some big dog from Harris County, here to bring those papers to us," Lawton said. "That's them over on Hack's desk."

Hack picked up the papers and rattled them again. "That's right," he said. "This is them."

"And exactly what are they?" Rhodes asked, thinking that this time he might actually get an answer, not that he really wanted one now. He was pretty sure he wasn't going to like it.

"We're bein' sued," Hack said.

"That's right," Lawton said. "Sued!" He shook his head. "I never been sued before in my whole life."

"Who, exactly, is being sued?" Rhodes asked Hack. "You and Lawton?"

"You're damn right. And you, and the county, and the commissioners, and ever'body they can think of."

"Everybody *who* can think of?"

Hack looked at Rhodes sorrowfully. "Who do you think?"

"I can't think of anyone," Rhodes said, trying to be patient.

"You remember that we had Little Barnes in here a while back?" Lawton said.

Rhodes remembered.

"And you remember how contentious him and his daddy always were?" Hack said.

Rhodes remembered that, too.

"Well, they're the ones suin' us," Hack said, shaking his head sadly. "You try to treat people right, and you see where it gets you."

"What are they suing us for?" Rhodes asked.

"A million dollars," Hack said.

"Apiece," Lawton said.

Rhodes laughed. He couldn't help it. He just started laughing. The idea that anyone could get a million dollars from him, much less from Hack and Lawton, was hilarious.

The other two didn't see the humor in it. They sat stony-faced and watched him laugh.

"I'm glad you think it's so funny," Hack said. "You won't be laughin' for long, though."

"Why not?" Rhodes said when he had gotten control of himself.

"'Cause I think they've got a good case," Hack said.

Rhodes didn't feel like laughing anymore. "Let's hear it," he said, and Hack finally told him.

What it came down to was that Barnes had turned out to be a pretty fair jailhouse lawyer, and with his father's help had gotten in touch with a real lawyer from Houston.

They were suing Hack, Lawton, and Rhodes for neglect. They were suing the county for conditions in the jail, specifically the fact that there was no supervised exercise program for prisoners, no air conditioning, no central heating, a leaky roof, and bad plumbing.

Rhodes was aware that, unfortunately, everything Barnes alleged was true, except the part about personal neglect. The jail was very old, after all, and though the county kept it up as best it could, it was certainly not a modern facility. There was no doubt they'd have to go to court, that the Commission on Jail Standards would investigate them, and that a number of changes would have to be made.

There might even have to be a new jail, though Rhodes didn't think there was any chance Barnes would collect any money.

"If we do get a new jail," Rhodes told Hack, "you could have that computer you've been wanting."

Lawton snickered, his mood suddenly improving. "He ain't worried about that computer. He's worried about that million dollars. 'Specially now that he's got himself a girlfriend."

14

Rhodes grinned. Hack had met Mrs. McGee not long ago as a result of a murder case.

"They been courtin' right regular," Lawton went on. "I figger we might have ourselves two weddin's before long."

Hack didn't think it was funny. "All right. You can laugh if you want to, but I bet you can't afford a lawyer any more than I can."

Lawton admitted that he couldn't. "I guess we can plead that we're poverty-struck. They'll have to let us off if we do that."

"I imagine the county will take care of things," Rhodes told them. "Most of those charges will never even go to court. There'll be a lot of bargaining back and forth before anything really happens."

He thought about what the county commissioners would say. If spending money were one of their favorite pastimes, there would have been a new jail long before now. He would have to talk to Jack Parry, the county judge, about things. That was the part he dreaded. The county fathers were not going to be pleased.

"For now, I wouldn't worry about it," Rhodes told Hack and Lawton. "If anything does come of it, nothing will happen for a long time. And if you don't have any money, they can't take it away from you."

Hack didn't look convinced. "They might try," he said. "And besides, that ain't the point. I don't like somebody suin' me for neglectin' them. I never neglected nobody."

"He's afraid they'll throw *him* in the jail," Lawton said. "Then he can't see his sweet patootie."

"If they throw him in jail, then he can sue us," Rhodes said.

That cheered Hack up a little. "Now that's not a bad idea. I'll take all Lawton has left after Little Barnes gets his million."

"They aren't going to get any of us for neglect, anyway, when it gets right down to it," Rhodes said. "That's just in

15

there for haggling. All the times I've been to the county asking for a new roof or for better cooling are on the record over at the commissioner's court, and some of the times I went before them, it was about requests you two had made for improvements. So there's no reason to worry about whether you were neglectful."

He hoped he was telling the truth. Even though he knew that nobody in that room was guilty of neglect, there was still that nagging little fear that some lawyer just might be able to get them mired in a lawsuit that would take years to straighten out. No matter how farfetched it seemed, it was always a possibility.

"I guess you'd better read the papers," Hack said, getting up and handing them to Rhodes.

Rhodes took them. He wasn't looking forward to reading them, but he knew that he had to. He started flipping through the pages.

Reading them thoroughly took him the rest of the morning.

At noon Rhodes went over to the courthouse. He liked the old building with its high ceilings and marble floors, but he didn't spend much time there, even though that was where his official office was located. There was a telephone there, but no one ever called. Anyone who wanted the sheriff called the jail, which is where Rhodes was most of the time when he was not out touring the county.

He went up the broad walk to the courthouse, looking up at the clear blue sky through the bare branches of the pecan trees. There were a few crisp brown leaves on the dead grass and on the walk, but there were no pecans. The county allowed anyone who wanted the nuts to pick them up, and they could hardly fall before someone grabbed them.

Rhodes's office was on the second floor, right above the county clerk's, one of the busiest offices in the building, since it was where everyone had to go to get their license plate stickers, to register to vote, transfer automobile titles, and perform similar items of important business.

Over his head were the courtrooms of both the county and district courts, as well as some of the judges' offices. There were some judges' offices on the second floor as well, but they were usually quiet.

That was the way Rhodes liked it. He could go to his official office and escape from the everyday worries of his job, and though he seldom did it, he liked the thought that the privacy was always there.

He also liked the fact that he could get a Dr Pepper in a glass bottle in the courthouse, about the only place in the county where that was still possible.

He got the soft drink from the old green-and-white machine and bought a package of Tom's cheese and peanut butter crackers from the newer red machine beside it. He thought ruefully of his waistline. How could someone who ate cheese crackers for lunch not lose weight? Well, *he* didn't. He had hoped to lose at least a few pounds before his marriage, but it didn't seem likely. He had even ridden his stationary bicycle a few times in the past week, but he knew that it was too little, too late.

He went to his office. Another thing he liked besides the quiet was that this room was completely uncluttered. There was, in fact, not a single thing on top of the desk except a few scratches left by Rhodes's heels when he propped them there while relaxing in his chair.

He added a few more scratches by sinking into the old leather office chair and putting his feet on the desk. He took a few satisfying sips of the icy cold Dr Pepper, ate two of the cheese crackers, and then picked up the phone and called Jack Parry, saying that he needed to talk.

Parry walked down from the third floor to Rhodes's

17

office, which was more private than his own. He opened the door and walked in without knocking. Rhodes took his feet off the desk.

"You going to back out?" Parry asked. He was a big man with only a fringe of close-cropped graying hair circling his bald head. He was chewing on an unlit cigar.

Rhodes was momentarily at a loss.

"Of the wedding," Parry said, settling himself into a worn leather armchair. "You remember the wedding, don't you?"

"Oh, the wedding." Rhodes remembered it, all right. He had asked Parry to perform the brief civil ceremony. He wondered if the lawsuit would interfere with the wedding. "No, it's not that."

"Didn't think it was, to tell the truth. That Dennis Naylor came to see me, too."

"Dennis Naylor?"

"That lawyer Little Barnes hired."

"Oh. Hack didn't tell me his name." Rhodes ate another cracker. "Just said he was a fancy lawyer."

Parry took the cigar out of his mouth and looked around for a place to put it. There wasn't one, so he stuck it back where it had been. "That's the kind of fella he was. He wouldn't give you the time of day if there was a way he could charge you for it."

That bothered Rhodes. "How do you think Barnes can afford him?"

"He's working on a contingency, I expect. I'd bet he came up here and got a good look at the jail, from the outside anyway, before he took on the case. Once he saw that dump, he figured he couldn't lose."

"I really appreciate you making me feel so much better about things," Rhodes said, taking a drink from the bottle of Dr Pepper.

Parry laughed. "Well, I can see where a man who's about

to tie the knot would be a little worried about finances. Ivy might not want to marry a pauper."

"It's not the money part that worries me. It's the part about the jail."

Parry grew serious. "That's pretty worrisome, all right." He looked around the office. "You got a trash can?"

Rhodes pulled the round green metal trash can from the kneehole of the desk. "Right here."

Parry stood up and leaned over the desk. Seeing the trash can, he took out the wet cigar and threw it in. It hit the bottom with a damp, dull splat.

Parry sat back down. "Now, where were we?"

"Worrying about the lawsuit. The part about the jail."

"Yeah, the jail. You know that place where you are is a rat's nest, don't you?"

"You preside at the commissioners' meetings," Rhodes reminded him.

"Yeah. So you know. And you've told us more than once." Parry leaned forward in his chair. "This is just between us, isn't it?"

"You know it is," Rhodes said.

"Well, just between us, we should've had a new jail in this county years ago. Probably a *lot* of years ago. It's just too bad that it's going to take something like this to make the commissioners get off their butts and take some action."

Rhodes wasn't sure he'd heard correctly. "You mean you think we'll be getting a new jail?"

"Damn right. We need one. I'm surprised the Jail Standards Commission didn't close us down a long time back. We'll get a new jail, all right, but not now, not right away. Hell, no. The commissioners will fight this suit tooth and nail, plead poverty, deny everything, do whatever they can to stall it, but it's inevitable. We'll get a jail, if for no other reason than that the court will probably order it."

Rhodes drained the Dr Pepper bottle and set it on the

19

desk. He couldn't believe it. A new jail. It didn't seem possible.

"Probably more deputies, too," Parry said. "Modern conveniences. You know the kind of thing. Television cameras for surveillance, air-conditioned cells . . ."

"Computers," Rhodes said.

"Right. Computers. All the latest gadgets."

"But not without a fight."

"Not without a hell of a fight, and not without a lot of kicking and screaming from the taxpayers." Parry smiled. "Most of the screaming will be directed at you, by the way. The commissioner will have to find someone to blame for the sorry condition the jail is in right now."

Rhodes ate the last cracker and the paper crackled as he crumpled it and tossed it in the trash can.

"I was afraid of that," he said.

THREE

Rhodes walked back over to the jail to see if anything that needed the sheriff's personal attention had come up.

Nothing had, but Lawton and Hack were a little more cheerful than they had been when Rhodes had left.

"We've been thinkin' about that supervised exercise program," Hack said. "We think it's a good idea."

"You do?" Rhodes said.

"That's right," Lawton said. "Me and Hack will be the ones to supervise it. We'll get the county to buy us one of those Jane Fonda workout tapes, and we'll watch it while the prisoners do their exercises."

"I thought you told me once that you didn't like her," Rhodes said. "Called her 'Hanoi Jane,' as I remember."

"Don't have anything to do with the way she does exercises," Lawton said.

"I don't think the county would go for it," Rhodes said. "Besides, we don't have a videotape player. We don't even have a TV set."

Hack nodded. "And that's just one more thing that's cruel and unusual about the punishment around here.

Whoever heard of a jail without a TV? They got 'em at all the prison farms, even got satellite dishes. It's a wonder we ain't had a riot. I'm surprised that Little Barnes didn't bring somethin' like that up in his lawsuit."

"Well, don't remind him," Rhodes said. "He'll probably add it in."

He waited to see if they had any more to say. When they didn't, he asked if there had been any calls.

"That Miz Stuart called from Sunny Dale," Hack said.

In the excitement over the lawsuit, Rhodes had forgotten all about Mr. Bobbit's teeth.

"What did she want?"

"Nothin' much. Said to tell you that she had herself a suspect, but she couldn't be dead certain. Wants to wait till supper to make sure. That make any sense to you?"

"Yes," Rhodes said. He told them about the missing teeth. "Either of you know Maurice Kennedy or Lloyd Bobbit?"

"You ought to remember that Bobbit fella," Hack said. "Course it's been a couple of years back, and maybe your memory ain't what it used to be."

Rhodes thought about the little man standing on the porch at the nursing home. He would have bet money that he'd never seen him before.

"I expect Lawton remembers, don't you Lawton?" Hack said.

"Sure do," Lawton said. "It was even in the big city papers."

The mention of the big city papers brought the incident back to Rhodes. He had never met Bobbit, but he had dealt with the daughter, the one who was giving Mr. Patterson trouble about the missing teeth.

Rhodes could sympathize with Patterson. Miss Bobbit had given him a bit of trouble, too.

"He went off to get his TV fixed," Hack said. "Disappeared off the face of the earth."

"For a day or two, anyhow," Lawton said. "That daughter of his tried to make it into a kidnap case, tried to get us to bring in the FBI."

"We didn't, though," Rhodes said.

"No, but the way she carried on, you prob'ly wanted to," Hack said. "Wanted us to keep it out of the papers, too."

"We couldn't do that, though," Lawton said. "It was big news when they found him."

"If those Houston cops hadn't been on the ball, she would've never seen the old guy again," Hack said, giving Rhodes a significant look. "They figured out who he was with a computer, you know."

"I know," Rhodes said. Hack never lost a chance to remind him of the value of state-of-the-art law enforcement techniques that were lacking in Blacklin County.

"Just put his license number in there, and knew who he was about a minute after that," Hack said. "Maybe ten seconds."

"I remember," Rhodes said.

Somehow, Mr. Bobbit, who had started out from his house in a green 1975 Chevy Bel-Air four-door, had wound up in Houston, a good three-and-a-half hours away, driving in the wrong direction on a one-way street in the middle of downtown. He had left his house more than a day earlier to take a portable thirteen-inch color TV into a Clearview shop for repair, and that was the last anyone heard of him until the police stopped him. The TV set was still in the backseat of the car.

The newspaper stories had referred to Bobbit as "a little mixed up about directions," and no one ever did find out exactly how he got to Houston, whether by working his way over to the interstate or by winding around the back roads. It was a small miracle that he had survived the trip, much less the time he had spent driving on the city streets.

According to what Bobbit said later, he had stopped and bought gas once, somewhere, but he had apparently not asked for directions to Clearview. Instead, he had asked how to get to Roy's TV. The attendant at the convenience store, or wherever it was the gas was bought, had no idea what the old man was talking about, so Bobbit had gotten back into his car and started driving. He had not eaten, and he had not had anything to drink except for an R. C. Cola that he bought at the convenience store. The empty R. C. can was lying in the front floor of the Chevy.

"Those Houston police treated me real nice," Mr. Bobbit told the newspapers. "Called my daughter up long distance and she come and got me."

It was not long after that episode that Mr. Bobbit had taken up residence in the Sunny Dale Nursing Home, where he had lived happily ever after, Rhodes assumed, until his teeth were stolen.

According to Hack, Maurice Kennedy had an even more colorful past.

"He was a real hellion in his day. Little before my time, but I used to hear stories about him when I was growin' up. There was even a story that he killed a fella one time."

"I heard about that, too," Lawton said. "Nobody ever proved it, though. Fella'd do a murder, though, he'd be one that'd steal teeth, I guess."

"The murder was a long time back," Hack said. "Sixty years, or thereabout. I don't recollect much of the story. Way I remember it, they never found a body."

"Probably doesn't have anything to do with the teeth," Rhodes said. "I've got to go out to the precinct three barn if there's nothing else happening."

"Nothin' that we know of," Hack said.

"I've got to go clean up the cells," Lawton said. "I don't want to be neglectin' anybody." He went out the door at the back of the office.

"You know Miz Wilkie works out there at the precinct barn now, don't you?" Hack said.

24

"Some of it's not true," Rhodes pointed out.

"I know that," Allen said. "You and those old boys at the jail never neglected anybody in your whole lives. Those prisoners eat better than half the county as long as Miz Stutts is feeding them, and they don't really suffer all that much from lack of exercise, either. I wonder if Little Barnes is going to claim that he was on a regular work-out schedule before he got himself arrested?"

"I doubt it," Rhodes said.

"Of course he's not. It's just a way he has of getting back at us for catching him. But he does have a point."

"I talked to Jack Parry. He thinks the county will get a new jail sooner or later."

"He's right. That old place you're in, it must be—what? Eighty years old?"

"About that," Rhodes said.

"Yeah. The Jail Standards people have been letting us slip by, but there's no air conditioning, and the roof leaks, and the plumbing backs up, and—"

"If it's so bad, why hasn't the county done anything before now?"

Allen sighed. "I know you've told us a lot of things that were wrong, and we didn't do much about them. Just slapped on a bandage, so to speak, and hoped we could get by for a few more years. It's not your fault."

"But I'll have to take the rap." Rhodes could feel his face getting hot. He liked Allen, and they went back a long way, but the longer Allen remained in office, the more like a politician he became. Rhodes didn't like being made the scapegoat.

"Now don't go getting your dandruff in an uproar," Allen said. "You won't have to take the blame." He sat forward in his chair and leaned on the desk. "Not all of it, anyway."

It was too bad, but Rhodes didn't entirely trust his old friend when he began getting chummy. "How much of it?" he said.

Rhodes admitted that he hadn't known.

"Well, she does. Got her a job answerin' the phone and bein' a secretary." Hack grinned. "Prob'ly had to do something to take her mind off you."

Mrs. Wilkie was a widow who had set her cap for Rhodes when his wife had died. She still hadn't quite given up hope, though the whole county knew that Rhodes was going to marry Ivy Daniel.

"I'll come back by before I go home," Rhodes told Hack. "If Miz Wilkie doesn't try to keep me. Let me know if anything comes up."

"I'll do that," Hack said.

The precinct barn was a huge steel building that was painted a strange shade of light greenish-blue. Rhodes thought the county had probably gotten the paint on sale. The building sat behind a cyclone fence on about a half acre of crushed gravel that shone white in the afternoon sun.

Beside the barn was another steel building of the same color. This one was really just a gigantic shed to house the precinct's pickups, road graders, backhoe machines, and dump trucks, all of which were painted an ugly school-bus yellow. Rhodes didn't count the openings in the shed, but there must have been at least ten. Most of the vehicles were missing, out hard at work on the county roads, he supposed.

He parked in front of the barn. The commissioner's office was in the front, separated from the rest of the building by a thin wall. In the back, there would be more vehicles under repair, damaged road signs being straightened and repainted, plans being laid for future road repairs. Rhodes could hear the clanging sound of metal being hammered. The office would be relatively quiet by comparison.

Rhodes entered the front door, hoping that Mrs. Wilkie wouldn't be there.

She was, however, though Rhodes, who had not seen her for a while, almost didn't recognize her. Her hair, which had been an improbable orange color the last time he saw her, had been allowed to return to its natural shade, a very light brown shot through with a great deal of gray. She was wearing very little makeup, and she was dressed in a businesslike suit of dark blue.

"Good afternoon, Sheriff," she said formally when he walked in. "Can I help you?" She was sitting at the reception desk near the door, looking efficient and capable.

Rhodes was slightly taken aback, but he said, "Good afternoon, Miz Wilkie. I came to talk to James Allen, if he's here."

"I'll see," she said. She picked up a beige telephone and punched three numbers. "Mr. Allen, the sheriff is here to see you." She listened for a moment, then hung up. "You can go right in."

Behind Mrs. Wilkie there was a partition with three doors in it. On one of the doors was a sign that said JAMES ALLEN, COUNTY COMMISSIONER, PRECINCT 3. That was the door Rhodes opened.

Allen got up from behind his desk and came around to shake Rhodes's hand. He was a big man, but he had very little fat on him. Rhodes envied him that, but he liked Allen anyway. They were the same age, and they had gone to high school together. Whenever he ran into a serious problem, one that the commissioners were going to have to deal with, Rhodes usually talked it over with Allen.

"Good to see you, Sheriff," Allen said, pumping Rhodes's arm. "How do you like my new secretary?"

"I almost didn't know her."

Allen laughed. He released Rhodes's hand and went to sit down. Rhodes sat in a straight-backed wooden chair facing the desk. He was glad to notice that this chair had a cushion in it, unlike the one in Patterson's office.

"She needed something to do," Allen said. "And Mary Sue had quit on me. Decided to spend her time raising her newest baby. Miz Wilkie was looking for a job, and she had the qualifications. My wife likes her, too. She thinks an older woman can be trusted."

Rhodes looked skeptical.

"You can tell Miz Wilkie's all business around here," Allen said. "I guess you already know this, but if she's romantically interested in anybody, you're still the one."

"I'm getting married on the twenty-seventh," Rhodes said. "To Ivy Daniel."

"I heard. Congratulations. But that doesn't change anything. Miz Wilkie's just trying a new tactic."

"A new tactic?"

"You're dating a career woman, aren't you? Someone who has a job, doesn't dye her hair, dresses professionally? Well, meet the new Miz Wilkie."

Rhodes didn't know what to say. As the silence stretched, he could hear the banging and pounding from the back of the barn.

Allen broke the spell. "Some of us got it, some of us don't. You've got it. Miz Wilkie can't resist you, any more than Ivy can."

Rhodes knew he was being kidded, but he didn't mind. Mrs. Wilkie might have changed her image for any number of reasons, but Rhodes didn't think he was one of them.

"Did you get a visit from a lawyer today?" he said, changing the subject.

"Matter of fact, I did," Allen said. "Looks like the county is about to get taken to court."

"You think you'll fight the suit, then?"

Allen laughed. "Hell, yes, we'll fight it. You don't think we're just going to admit to anything in that lawsuit, do you? Even if it is all true."

26

27

"Maybe a little bit. Not much. The county hasn't had the money to do anything till now, and we've got a lot of fiscal conservatives on the commissioners' court."

Right, Rhodes thought. *All of them.*

"Where's the money going to come from?" he asked.

"The power plant," Allen told him. "The one they're building down below Braceville. That's going to bring in the tax money, boy, let me tell you."

He was beaming, the way Rhodes suspected that any politician would beam when talking about bringing in bundles of tax money that the local taxpayers wouldn't feel coming out of their pockets.

"That big lake that goes with it," Allen went on, "that'll help, too. The new jail won't be the end of the changes we'll see around here."

The county needed a new jail, all right, but the thought of all the changes made Rhodes uncomfortable. Now he knew what Parry meant about more deputies and all the rest. The county was going to be different, and it might be that the difference wouldn't necessarily improve things.

"I don't think we ever got it clear about how much I'm going to be blamed," he said.

"All right, all right," Allen said. "You have to admit that you didn't exercise the prisoners."

"Where would I do that?" Rhodes said.

"Good point. I guess you couldn't very well do it in the middle of the street. How about that leaky roof?"

"We might check the weather records. I don't think it even rained while Little Barnes was in jail, at least not enough to make the roof leak."

"Damn! I didn't even think of that. Who do we check with?"

"They keep records at the newspaper office," Rhodes said.

29

"I don't know if I want to get close to the newspaper office right now," Allen said. "What with the lawsuit and all."

Rhodes didn't blame him. "I can ask Ivy to check," he said.

Allen smiled. "You know, you're pretty smart for a Texas sheriff. I guess you won't get much of the blame after all."

"Good," Rhodes said. But he still wasn't satisfied. "It's not just me I'm worried about, though. I don't want Hack and Lawton to take any of the blame, either."

"Don't worry. The more I think about this, the more I think it might not even go to court. I bet that fancy lawyer didn't think about checking the weather records. No telling where else he got careless. You can tell Hack and Lawton to put their minds at ease."

"I'll do that," Rhodes said. He got up to go.

"What's the movie?" Allen said. "The one where Marlon Brando plays a Texas sheriff?"

"*The Chase*," Rhodes said. He knew almost as much about movies as he did about being sheriff, especially old, bad movies.

"That's the one," Allen said. "There's a fella in it they call Bubber."

"Robert Redford," Rhodes said.

"Robert Redford. I'll be damned." Allen thought for a second. "You ever know anybody called Bubber?"

"Never," Rhodes said.

"Me neither. Bubba, maybe, but not Bubber. You ever know a bunch of people as crazy as the ones in that movie?"

"Never did," Rhodes said.

Allen nodded agreement. "Me neither. Not around here. So you can tell your boys not to worry. We won't string 'em up for neglect."

"I'm sure that will make them feel a lot better," Rhodes

said. "I'd hate to think I'd get as beat up as Marlon Brando did while I was trying to protect them."

"That's another thing you don't have to worry about," Allen assured him.

"Good," Rhodes said, but for some reason he still didn't feel a whole lot better.

FOUR

Rhodes left Allen's office and went out past Mrs. Wilkie, who was still doing a good job of looking coolly professional. Maybe she really was. Rhodes didn't intend to linger and investigate.

When he got back to the jail, he didn't have time to tell Lawton and Hack not to worry. The place was in an uproar.

There were five people in the office, making it somewhat crowded, and most of them were yelling. Hack was there, of course, and Lawton. The other three were deputy Ruth Grady and two men, one of whom was holding a double-barreled shotgun.

No one turned to look at Rhodes when he entered, so he slammed the door as hard as he could.

There was a sudden silence, and Ruth Grady said, "Here's the sheriff now."

Everyone else started talking then, and Rhodes held up his hands. "Just be quiet for a minute," he said. "Let's get this sorted out."

Hack wanted to say something, but Rhodes shook his

head at him and said, "I guess these are Deputy Grady's prisoners. Let her tell it."

Hack clamped his mouth shut and glared at Lawton, who had started to laugh. Lawton was glad that if he wasn't going to get to tell things, at least Hack, who had tried to jump in before him, wouldn't be the one to get to tell them either.

"Who are these two men?" Rhodes asked. "And why does one of them have a shotgun?"

"The man with the gun is Will Foy," Ruth said. She was short, stout, and even-tempered. Her own sidearm was in its holster. "He's got the gun because he was making a citizen's arrest of Bert Eoff, the other gentleman there."

Foy stared at Rhodes defiantly, as if daring him to do anything about the gun. He was about sixty years old, a short man, not much taller than Ruth Grady. He had watery blue eyes, and it appeared that he had a dip of snuff, or "smokeless tobacco" as the ad men called it these days, in his pursed mouth.

Eoff looked to be about the same age as Foy, but he was taller, nearly six feet, and he did not look defiant. In fact, he looked about as guilty as anyone who had ever come into the jail. His head was lowered, his eyes were downcast, and he was shuffling his feet nervously.

"What was the arrest for?" Rhodes asked.

"I coulda shot him," Foy said. "I shoulda done it. I—"

"Not you," Rhodes said. "I was talking to the deputy."

"Oh," Foy said.

"Go ahead, Ruth," Rhodes said.

"Well, I got a call from Hack that there was a disturbance over on Oak Street. Some of the neighbors called it in. When I got there, Mr. Foy was marching Mr. Eoff down the middle of the street, with that shotgun sticking in the middle of his back."

Eoff did not raise his head. He mumbled something that Rhodes couldn't quite hear.

"You'll have to speak up, Mr. Eoff," Rhodes said.

Eoff tilted his head up slightly. "Yes. I was trespassing. I'm guilty, Sheriff. Lock me up."

"That ain't all," Foy said. "Tell 'em *why* you were trespassin'."

"I was cutting down a tree."

"A tree?" Rhodes said. "On your own property?"

"No." Eoff's voice was sad. "It was in Mr. Foy's yard."

"That's probably murder," Foy said. "He killed the tree. That's murder, ain't it?"

"No," Rhodes said. "Criminal mischief, maybe. Why were you cutting down the tree, Mr. Eoff?"

"It was in the way."

"In the way of what?"

"Of his damn satellite dish," Foy said, and this time Rhodes let him go on. "Sheriff, that tree was a giant oak, older than I am. My daddy planted that tree when he was just a young man. Why, I bet that tree's eighty years old, and this bastard . . ." He looked at Ruth. "Pardon me, ma'am. Anyway, he cut it down, or as good as. One little push, and it's gone. I heard this noise, and I didn't know what it was at first. Then I said to myself, 'that's a chain saw, that's what that is, and it sounds like it's right in my yard.' Well, it was a chain saw, all right, and by the time I got out there, Eoff and his McCullouch were almost done with the job."

"Is all that true, Mr. Eoff?"

Eoff was studying the floor again. He nodded. "It's true. I was trespassing, and I cut down the tree. Lock me up, Sheriff."

Rhodes had never seen a prisoner who was so repentant. "You mean you really did what he just said? You cut down the tree to get better TV reception?"

"That's the damndest thing of all," Foy broke in. "Do you know what he said to me when I caught him?" Foy looked around questioningly.

35

No one knew, but by now they were all interested in finding out.

"He said, 'Now I can get The Nashville Network,' that's what he said."

"Is that right, Mr. Eoff?" Rhodes asked.

"That's right, Sheriff. I'm addicted to TV, is what it is. You know, like that ballplayer who was addicted to sex? He was on 'Oprah' one day. Or maybe it was 'Geraldo.' Anyhow, I'm not that interested in sex, but I'm addicted to watching TV. I have to be able to get everything, and I couldn't get TNN. Well, I could, but it wasn't a very good picture. And that tree was in the way. So I just decided to cut it down."

"Without asking Mr. Foy?"

Eoff shot a sidelong glance at his neighbor. "He would've just said no. So I didn't ask him. I'm guilty, Sheriff."

"Trespasser!" Mr. Foy yelled. "I shoulda shot you! My daddy—"

"That's enough of that," Rhodes said.

Foy hushed again.

"Lawton, we'd better lock Mr. Eoff up until he can post bond. I'll talk to Mr. Foy about the charges."

"Do you have satellite TV?" Mr. Eoff asked Lawton.

Lawton laughed. "We don't have no TV at all."

"What?" Eoff wailed. "No TV at all?" He looked wildly over his shoulder. "Wait a minute! I can't stand this! I'm a TV addict, I told you! I've got to have it!"

"Not here, you don't," Hack said.

Eoff had stopped dead in his tracks. Now he refused to move. "I'm not going anywhere that doesn't have TV!"

"Yes, you are," Rhodes said.

"Then he's going too," Eoff said, pointing at Foy. "I'm filing charges against him. Assault with a deadly weapon. That's as bad as trespassing!"

Foy made a run for him. "You can't charge me with nothin'! I'm a member of the NRA!"

Ruth Grady grabbed Foy's arm and spun him around. "Hold it, buster," she said.

"I can't stay here!" Eoff wailed. "I've got to have a TV. I thought jailhouses were supposed to have TV for the prisoners. If I don't have TV, I'll sue."

"Get in line," Hack said.

"I knew I shoulda shot him," Foy said. Ruth Grady was still holding his arm.

"You won't be here long," Rhodes told Eoff. "Just long enough for the judge to set bail. You won't miss your TV much at all."

"That's right," Foy said. "Send the criminals right back out on the streets! All the jails in this state might's well have revolvin' doors, the way the crooks and killers get turned back out."

"That's enough of that, Mr. Foy," Rhodes said. "You can go on home now. I'll just hold onto this shotgun as evidence. You can have it back after the case comes up in court."

"A man's got a right to his guns," Foy said.

"I bet you got plenty more of 'em at home," Lawton said, no longer able to keep out of it.

"That's probably true," Rhodes agreed. "Take him on home, Ruth. We'll book Mr. Eoff and then he can go to his cell."

Ruth kept her hold on Foy's arm and tugged him toward the door while Lawton took Eoff over to the table where the fingerprint kit and camera were.

Things were almost back to normal when the phone rang.

Hack answered. Rhodes could hear someone on the other end of the line talking very loudly. More trouble.

"Calm down," Hack said. "I can't understand you." He listened for a minute longer. "All right. All right. The sheriff's here. You can talk to him."

Rhodes went over to his own desk and picked up the extension. "Hello," he said.

"Sheriff? This is Earlene over at Sunny Dale and you better get over here right away, we've got some real trouble, Mr. Patterson said to call, you come right—"

"Just a minute, Earlene," Rhodes said. He looked at Hack, who shrugged. Evidently he hadn't been able to calm Earlene down.

Rhodes counted to ten, slowly. Then he spoke into the phone. "Earlene? What seems to be the trouble?"

Earlene had gotten a grip on herself during the wait. "We have a problem here at Sunny Dale," she said. "Mr. Patterson wanted me to call you." She took a deep breath and let it out slowly. "There's been a death."

"A death?" Rhodes didn't see anything unusual in that. There were a number of people at Sunny Dale who seemed to be just passing the time until they died. He had seen a lot of them.

"It's Mr. Bobbit," Earlene said, as if that explained everything.

"Mr. Bobbit is dead?" Rhodes had to admit that Mr. Bobbit's death would be unusual. The old man had seemed a little vague about things, but he had been very much alive that morning.

"That's right," Earlene said. "He's dead. Can you come right on out here? Mr. Patterson's pretty upset."

"Did he have a heart attack?"

"Mr. Patterson? No, but he's about to if you don't get out here."

"I meant Mr. Bobbit," Rhodes said.

"No, he didn't have any heart attack," Earlene said. "Somebody's gone and killed him."

It didn't take long for Rhodes to get to Sunny Dale. He hadn't been able to get much more out of Earlene, but it seemed fairly certain that there was no mistake, that Mr. Bobbit had really been killed and had not died from natural causes. She assured Rhodes that a doctor had already been called.

Rhodes could tell when he entered the nursing home that something had happened. It was in the air, a kind of hushed tension that you could almost feel.

Earlene was at the desk. "It's right down the hall there," she said, pointing. She didn't tell him what "it" was, but he had a pretty good idea.

As he walked down the hall past the Stuarts' room, someone hissed at him. He looked in the door and saw the old couple sitting at their little table. They weren't playing cards, however. They were both looking at him.

He stepped in, and Mrs. Stuart said, "We heard about it, Sheriff. You think whoever killed him is the one that got his teeth?"

"I don't know anything yet," Rhodes said. "I haven't talked to anyone except Earlene, and I didn't find out much from her."

"I bet it was the teeth," Mr. Stuart said. "That's a pretty low thing, Sheriff, killing a man for his teeth."

"You're right about that, if that's what it was," Rhodes said. "I think you better let me investigate that bit of business from now on, Miz Stuart. It might turn out to be dangerous."

He didn't really think there was any connection between the missing teeth and the death. It seemed too farfetched. But you could never be sure.

The old woman agreed to let Rhodes handle things, and he went on down the hall to Bobbit's room. Mr. Patterson was standing just inside the door, and there was another man beside the bed.

The other man was Dr. Pearsall, who saw most of the nursing home patients. He was fifty years old, and his thick shock of completely white hair gave him the kind of distinguished appearance that people automatically trusted. Rhodes had heard that he was a good doctor.

"Thank goodness you've come, Sheriff," Mr. Patterson said. "This is awful, just awful."

Rhodes stepped past Patterson, who didn't offer to shake hands this time, and into the room. There was a body lying on the bed, but it was partially obscured by Dr. Pearsall.

"What happened?" Rhodes asked.

"Someone killed Mr. Bobbit," Mr. Patterson said, just as Dr. Pearsall stepped away from the bed.

As soon as Rhodes got a good look at the body, he saw why Mr. Patterson was so upset. There wasn't any doubt that murder had been done in the Sunny Dale Nursing Home.

Rhodes could see only Mr. Bobbit's head, but it was in a white plastic grocery bag that had been tied around his neck. In trying to breathe, Mr. Bobbit had sucked the bag in around his features, and it looked like a grotesque white mask.

"He's tied under the spread, too," Dr. Pearsall said in a deep voice perfectly in keeping with his appearance. "He couldn't get his hands free to take the bag off, and he couldn't get off the bed."

He pulled the bedspread back, and Rhodes could see that Mr. Bobbit was tied to the twin bed by two sheets, one that went around his chest and one that went across his legs at the ankles.

"Where did the sheets come from?" Rhodes asked.

"The closet, probably," Mr. Patterson said. "We always leave a spare set in the room."

"What happened, at a guess," Dr. Pearsall said, "is that someone came in and found him asleep, tied him to the bed, and popped on the bag. It wouldn't have taken long, and while Mr. Bobbit was generally in good health, he wasn't particularly strong."

Rhodes thought of the old man as he had been that morning, his thin neck sticking out of the shirt collar.

"He wouldn't have been able to put up much of a struggle," Dr. Pearsall went on. He nodded toward the bag. "And he wouldn't have been able to call out."

Rhodes had heard a sample of Mr. Bobbit's lung power. "Why not?" he said.

"Every time he sucked in a breath, he sucked in the bag," Pearsall said.

Patterson shuddered. "This is just awful. Whatever can I tell Miss Bobbit?"

Rhodes looked at him. "The truth," he said.

"But this is murder!" Patterson said. He looked at Rhodes. "You've got to find out who did it."

Rhodes sighed. "That's what they pay me for."

CHAPTER
FIVE

Rhodes was wondering how he was going to earn his salary this time when Earlene came into the room, a frightened look on her face.

"Mr. Patterson," she said, "can I see you for a minute?" She was trying not to look at Mr. Bobbit.

"What's the matter?" Patterson snapped. He was clearly not in a mood to be trifled with by the hired help. Mr. Bobbit's death had upset him more than he would have liked to admit. It wasn't that death was so unusual in Sunny Dale, Rhodes thought; it was the way this particular death had occurred.

Earlene didn't seem eager to talk in front of Rhodes and the doctor, but since Patterson insisted, she blurted out her news. "Mr. Kennedy's missing!"

"Ohmigod," Patterson said, looking around for a chair. There was one not far from Mr. Bobbit's bed. It had a straight metal back and a red vinyl seat. Mr. Patterson sat down in it and put his head in his hands.

"That wouldn't be Maurice Kennedy, would it?" Rhodes said.

Earlene turned to him. "Yes, it would. How'd you know?"

"Just a guess. How long has he been gone?"

"I don't know," Earlene confessed. "It was time for him to take his afternoon medication, and one of the nurses took it to his room. He wasn't there."

"Did you check the other rooms?" Dr. Pearsall asked.

"Why of course we did. But he's not in any of them. He's just gone."

Pearsall looked at Rhodes. "You think there's any connection?"

Rhodes shook his head. "Probably not." He didn't want to start any idle speculation.

He walked over to Mr. Patterson. "I'll get out a bulletin on Mr. Kennedy. He won't be far."

Mr. Patterson didn't even look up. He was probably worrying about the black eye all this was going to give his nursing home, Rhodes thought.

"You'd better call Clyde Ballinger," Rhodes told Pearsall. "Have him take care of the body." Ballinger was the local funeral director.

"I've already called him," Earlene said.

On his way out, Rhodes stopped in the Stuarts' room. "We've just heard," Mrs. Stuart said.

"Heard what?" Rhodes asked.

"About Maurice Kennedy," Mr. Stuart said. "What'd you think?"

Rhodes couldn't believe how efficient the grapevine was. There wasn't even anyone in the room who could have told them. "You have any idea where he's gone?" he asked.

"Not a'tall," Mr. Stuart said. "You think he killed Bobbit?"

"I don't know anything yet. I'm surprised someone hasn't told you, though."

"We know just about ever'thing that goes on in this place, and you better believe it," Mr. Stuart said. "Cept who took those teeth and who killed Mr. Bobbit."

"And I was workin' on the teeth," Mrs. Stuart said. "I think Maurice Kennedy took 'em, myself."

"You don't know that, though," Mr. Stuart pointed out. "I'm not payin' any three thousand dollars out till you can prove it."

"We didn't have anything for lunch that needed teeth," Mrs. Stuart said. "Just that brown mushy stuff."

"That was chipped beef," her husband said.

"Whatever it was, you didn't need any teeth for it," she said. "But it was a little stringy."

"You don't have any idea where Maurice Kennedy might have gotten off to, do you?" Rhodes asked them.

"Not a one," Mr. Stuart said. "He'd have to walk, though, 'less he stole somebody's car. Wouldn't put it past him, either."

"Why?" Rhodes said.

" 'Cause that Maurice Kennedy was a real hellraiser in his day," Mr. Stuart said. Then he looked at his wife. " 'Scuse my language, honey."

She shook her head. "It's what comes of reading those rough books. That Mickey Spillane uses such crude words."

"It's nothin' compared to what that King fella does!" Mr. Stuart said. "Why I bet he uses the F-word more than Mickey Spillane ever did!"

"That's beside the point," Mrs. Stuart said primly.

Rhodes interrupted before they got too far off the track. "What were you going to say about Maurice Kennedy?"

Mr. Stuart struggled to get his mind back to the topic. "Maurice Kennedy?"

"About how he was a . . . how he was pretty wild in his day," Rhodes said.

"Oh. Yeah. Well, he was, and that's a fact. There was this

45

girl named Peggy Rainey, pretty little thing, blond hair, cute figure—"

He broke off when his wife poked him in the ribs. "How do you know so much about her, you old goat?"

Mr. Stuart looked to Rhodes for help. Rhodes looked the other way.

"Well, ever'body knew her," Mr. Stuart said. "She was a popular girl, but she was a little younger than me. I was never interested in her, if that's what you mean."

"Ha," Mrs. Stuart said.

"Well, I wasn't. She was pretty, but she had a wild streak. I wasn't ever interested in that kind of a girl, myself."

"Ha," Mrs. Stuart repeated.

"Maurice Kennedy," Rhodes said helpfully.

Mr. Stuart looked at him gratefully. "Oh. Yeah. Him and Louis Horn both liked Peggy Rainey, but she seemed to favor Louis. His daddy was a big landowner around here in those days, and ever'body thought they might strike oil on his land. They struck it lots of places, but they never did strike it on his. They started callin' him Dry Hole Horn, as I remember."

Mr. Stuart's eyes dimmed as he wandered somewhere back into the past that was still alive in his head.

"I didn't know that girl, but I remember the rest of this story," Mrs. Stuart said. "Dry Hole Horn's son disappeared one night after a dance in town. There was a big storm that night, and some folks thought he got struck by lightning. They found his car down by the river, and some other folks thought he might've got out for some reason or another and drowned."

Mr. Stuart came back from wherever he had been. "But most folks thought Maurice Kennedy killed him. Dry Hole Horn raised a big stink about it, and the sheriff even arrested Maurice, but they never proved anythin'. Never found the body, neither. Too bad Mr. Bobbit's dead. He and

46

Maurice Kennedy go 'way back. If anybody could've told you about those days, he could."

"Who was the sheriff then?" Rhodes asked.

Mr. Stuart thought about it. "Musta been Reb Trotter. Lordy, that was a long time back. Sixty years, if it was a day."

Rhodes would check the old records in his courthouse office. It was possible that there was still something there about the Kennedy business. No one ever seemed to throw anything like that away.

"I'll look into it," he told the Stuarts. "Meanwhile, you forget about those teeth. They may turn up when we search Mr. Bobbit's room."

"Bet they don't," Mrs. Stuart said, and she turned out to be correct.

Before he left the nursing home, Rhodes talked to Earlene one more time. He wanted to know who had visited the rooms that afternoon.

She was sitting behind the reception desk, filing her nails. She seemed to have recovered from the shock of Mr. Bobbit's death.

Rhodes asked if Mr. Bobbit's daughter had been informed of her father's death.

"Mr. Patterson takes care of things like that personally," Earlene said.

Rhodes assumed that meant "yes," so he asked about the visitors for the afternoon.

"Well, we don't exactly keep records on that," Earlene said. "It's not like there's a book they have to sign or anything."

Rhodes told her that he was aware of that. "But you're sitting right out here. You can see whoever comes in or goes out, can't you?"

Earlene reached down to the floor and came up with a

brown leather purse. She unzipped a compartment in it and stuck the nail file inside.

"There's usually two of us out here," She said when she had put the purse back down on the floor.

"I know that," Rhodes said. A black woman named Linda usually helped out at the desk. "Where's Linda?"

"She's out with the flu. We can't have anybody with the flu comin' in to work. If all these old folks came down with the flu, we'd be in a real mess."

Rhodes understood that. "But what does that have to do with your seeing who came in or went out?"

Earlene looked at him defensively. "Well, if you must know, I went back to the storeroom for a cigarette. A gal's got a right to have a break, you know?"

"How long were you back there?"

"Not long. I didn't even smoke the whole thing, either time."

"You were back there twice?"

"Well, what's wrong with that? Mr. Patterson can't expect me just to sit here all day and never even get a break, can he?" Earlene was obviously worried. "You won't tell him, will you?"

"Not unless it makes a difference to the murder," Rhodes said. "Why don't you just make me a list of the people you can remember seeing while you were here. That might be all I need."

Earlene took a note pad from beside the phone and began writing on it with a Bic pen that she took from the desk top. When she finished there were only six names on the list, and Rhodes did not recognize any of them except for that of Brenda Bobbit, Mr. Bobbit's daughter.

"Do you remember what time any of these people came in?" he asked.

Earlene looked as if she couldn't believe he had asked such a stupid question. "Of course not," she said.

Rhodes folded the paper and stuck it in his shirt pocket.

If called upon, Earlene was going to make a wonderful witness.

Rhodes stopped his car behind Ballinger's Funeral Home, which had once been one of the more elegant mansions in Clearview. Clyde Ballinger had his office in what had been the servants' quarters in back of the main building.

Rhodes got out of the car and knocked on the door.

"Come on in," Ballinger called.

Rhodes opened the door and went in. Ballinger, who would not have fit most people's idea of a funeral director, being a cheerful man who was always ready with a joke or a story, was sitting at his desk reading an old paperback with a lurid cover. He laid it on the desk when the sheriff came in.

Rhodes glanced at the title and saw that it was *The Lady Kills*, by Bruno Fischer. The cover showed a blond woman holding a shotgun on someone who was standing out of the picture. All that could be seen of the person was a hand holding a coiled bullwhip.

Ballinger saw Rhodes looking at the book. "It's not as kinky as it looks," he said. Then he shook his head. "Used to be you could find books like this all the time, at garage sales or used book stores, but they're just about gone now. Too many people collecting them, and it's pushed the prices up. I didn't pay more'n a dime for most of these." He indicated the shelves of the office, which held other titles by any number of writers Rhodes had never heard anyone except Ballinger express any enthusiasm for, writers like Richard Telfair, John Flagg, Hallam Whitney.

"You have any more by this Fischer?" Rhodes asked.

Ballinger got up and looked on the shelves. He took off a copy of *The Lustful Ape* and handed it to Rhodes. "How's that for a great title?" he asked.

49

Rhodes looked the book over and handed it back to Ballinger. The cover, which showed an apparently frightened woman wearing a slip and standing in front of a rumpled bed, was not nearly as interesting as the other one.

"Has Miss Bobbit been by yet?" Rhodes asked as Ballinger put the book back on the crowded shelf.

"She sure has," Ballinger said. "And she's pretty upset. I'd hate to be in Patterson's shoes, or yours either. It would have been bad enough if the old man had just died of natural causes, but this is really something. Dr. White's having a look at the body now, but it looks like a simple case of suffocation to me. I'm not a doctor, but that's what it looks like to me. Now if Carella and the guys in the 87th got hold of a case like this, you might think it was the Deaf Man on the loose, killing an old man like that."

"Most of the men in Sunny Dale can hear as well as you and I can," Rhodes said. He had heard Ballinger go on about the 87th precinct before.

"What I meant was—" Ballinger began.

"I know what you meant. Did Miss Bobbit say anything about her plans?"

"To hear her tell it, she's going to sue Patterson and run you out of town on a rail if you don't catch whoever killed her daddy. And I gather that you better do it quick."

Rhodes had been afraid of that. After Hack's reminder, he had recalled that Miss Bobbit could be a real nuisance if she chose to be. And she probably would.

"I'd better go talk to Dr. White," he said.

Rhodes did not learn much from Dr. White that he had not already known. Mr. Bobbit had indeed died from suffocation. There were no marks on his body, other than those caused by the fact that he had been bound to the bed by the sheets.

"No blows to the head, no signs of a struggle?" Rhodes asked.

"None at all," Dr. White said. "He might have been asleep when he was tied to the bed. That would account for it."

"Any sign of drugs?"

"None of that either. Apparently he wasn't taking any medication at Sunny Dale."

"And no teeth, either," Rhodes said.

"No teeth," Dr. White agreed. "I'd say he'd been using false teeth until recently, however."

"He told me earlier today that someone stole his teeth," Rhodes said.

Dr. White shook his head. "I hope I don't ever wind up in a place where somebody might steal my teeth."

"So do I," Rhodes said. "So do I."

Six

Rhodes wanted to talk to the people on Earlene's list, but first he drove back to the jail to check on the bulletin he had called in to Hack from Sunny Dale in case anyone had found Maurice Kennedy. He could have called in on his radio, but he wanted to see if there was anything else going on that he needed to take a personal hand in.

As it turned out, there was.

"James Allen's been tryin' to call you for about an hour," Hack said when Rhodes walked through the door.

"Did he say what he wanted?"

"Nope, but he sure didn't sound happy. I could almost hear him sweatin' over the phone."

Uh-oh, Rhodes thought.

"You reckon it's about that lawsuit?" Hack asked.

"Could be," Rhodes said. "What about Eoff?"

"Bailed out. You think we're gonna have to pay that million dollars?"

"I'm not. I still don't have the money," Rhodes didn't want to talk about it. If Allen sounded worried, it couldn't have been good news. "What about the bulletin on Maurice Kennedy. Did you send it out?"

Hack thumbed through a stack of penciled notes on his desk and came up with the one he was looking for. "You bet I did. All the deputies know about him, for all the good that'll do. I sent it on to the state highway boys, too. You think he's got himself a car?"

"If he does, he didn't steal it at Sunny Dale," Rhodes said. "And he didn't have one of his own. He got any family here in town?"

"Not that I know of," Hack said. "If he had a car, and if we knew the license number, we could send that in and the state boys could get it on the computer. They'd get him then, I bet. Them computers are somethin'."

"Never mind the computers right now. You know any of these people?" He handed Earlene's list to Hack.

Hack went over the names. "Miz Bobbit, I know her, all right. Dave Foley, never head of him. Lyle Everett, never heard of him, either. I think I know Andy West, though. His daddy used to run that fillin' station out on the Obert Road. Had a stroke last year, and he's probably out there in Sunny Dale himself."

Rhodes remembered the station. It had closed several years before. West had been able to keep it going for years after the gas crisis had passed by making it a self-service facility, putting in a few groceries, and hiring a full-time mechanic.

"Where does his son live?" Rhodes asked.

"Out there in back of the old station, I think," Hack said. "Works in the furniture factory. Why?"

"Those are the people Earlene saw come in this afternoon," Rhodes said. "You know of any connection between the Wests and Mr. Bobbit?"

"Nope. That don't mean there ain't one, though."

"All right. I'll talk to both of them later. I guess I'd better see what James Allen wants first, though."

It wasn't a chore he was looking forward to.

It turned out to be even worse than he thought.

Since he preferred to talk to people face to face rather than on the telephone, he drove back out to the precinct barn. It was getting late, and the shadows were lengthening across the gravel yard. The wind had picked up a little and had a bit of a bite in it.

Rhodes hunched his shoulders, walked to the door, and went in. It was much warmer inside, almost too warm. The small window in the front wall was covered with moisture. Mrs. Wilkie was still there at her desk, and she looked up, surprised to see Rhodes again.

"Why, hello, Sheriff," she trilled. "How can I help you?"

There was probably no invitation at all in her words, but Rhodes couldn't help thinking that there was a note of hope there, as if he might have come to see, not the commissioner, but her.

"Is Mr. Allen in?" he said.

"Oh. Yes, I believe he is," Mrs. Wilkie said. She picked up the beige phone and announced Rhodes.

Rhodes went into Allen's office, noting that his old friend did not look happy. The commissioner did not even get up and offer to shake hands.

"What's the problem?" Rhodes asked, sitting in the wooden chair and expecting the worst.

Allen leaned forward. "I've been getting a lot of calls this afternoon," he said. "The news is definitely not good."

"The other commissioners?" Rhodes said. "They've been calling?"

"Them, too," Allen said.

"Who else?"

"The problem's money," Allen said, evading the question.

"I thought the power plant was going to take care of all that," Rhodes said.

"Well, that's the problem. We're not the only ones getting sued."

"You want to explain that?"

"The power company's getting sued, too. They built that big newkular plant down on the coast, but one of the cities they were going to sell that newkular power to has sued 'em."

"I read about that," Rhodes said. "But what does that have to do with us?"

"Well, the power company has offered the city a big percentage of the coal plant here in Blacklin County to replace what they owned of the newkular plant."

Rhodes didn't see the connection. He said so.

"Well, hell," Allen said. "If the city gets the percentage, they won't have to pay taxes on it."

"Oh," Rhodes said.

"And that ain't all," Allen said.

Rhodes didn't think he wanted to hear the rest, but Allen told him anyway.

"See, what the other commissioners told me is that there's another tax thing. The way it works, the power plant paid us a lot of money last year, and we used most of that to fix up some of the roads and to get the courthouse renovation project started."

Rhodes didn't recall seeing any renovation going on. When he mentioned that, Allen said, "Well, we haven't really gotten *started* on it yet, but the bids have been let. They'll be getting an elevator over there, for one thing, and some ramps out front. We gotta make things more accessible for the handicapped; it's a federal law or something."

"I remember now," Rhodes said. "But why can't we use this year's money for the jail?"

" 'Cause there might not be that much money. See, the way it works is that the power plant depreciated all its equipment, and they took a lot of coal out of the ground, so that depreciated the value of the land."

Rhodes didn't like what Allen was saying, but he could see how it worked.

He started to say something, but Allen didn't give him a chance. "And that's still not all."

Rhodes leaned back in his chair and awaited the rest. The hard wood pressed into his backbone, but he hardly noticed. He was getting numb.

"OK," he said. "Go ahead and tell me."

"Well, see, the way it is, is they'll go on depreciating a whole lot every year. That means—"

"That means there'll be less and less tax money coming in every year that passes," Rhodes finished for him.

"You got it," Allen told him.

"So what does all that mean?"

"It means that building a new jail won't be as easy as I told you it would. There's gonna have to be a bond election, of course, which would've passed easy if we'd had the money from the power plant. Now it won't be so easy."

"And I guess the lawsuit is a little more important than it was, too."

"Damn right. Maybe that lawyer will listen to reason, though."

"Sure he will," Rhodes said. "And Ed McMahon will bring ten million dollars right to my very own door this week."

"You send in those things, too?" Allen asked.

"No," Rhodes said. "But maybe I better get started doing it."

It was nearly five-thirty when Rhodes left Allen's office. Mrs. Wilkie had already locked her desk and gone home, which was not the disappointment to Rhodes that she might have wanted it to be.

He went outside and got in his car, started it, and turned on the heater. While he waited for it to warm up, he got out the paper with the list of names on it. He was surprised to find that he could hardly read it.

It was almost dark now, and that probably accounted for it. The sun was no more than half a red ball off in the west, just about to sink out of sight. Rhodes turned on the car's interior light.

That helped, but not much. Rhodes wondered if he could have read the names at all if he had not pretty well memorized them. He'd been putting off buying a pair of reading glasses, but it was getting more and more obvious that he was going to have to make the purchase.

He thought about the list. He could drive on out to Obert Road and look for West, but Miss Bobbit was closer. As much as he hated the thought of it, he was going to have to talk to her sooner or later. It might as well be sooner.

The heater was blowing warm air now. Rhodes put the car in reverse and backed out of the parking lot.

Miss Bobbit lived in what people in Clearview still called the "new addition," an area just within the city limits where a developer had begun building new homes about ten years before. There were now eighteen or twenty homes there, not exactly the rapid burst of development that the originator of the idea had hoped for, but then Clearview had never experienced much of a population explosion.

The Bobbit house was one of the newer ones, set back from the street and fronted by a wide lawn. It was a lot of lawn for a new house, but when Rhodes looked the place over he decided that Miss Bobbit must have bought two lots.

Rhodes wondered who kept the grass cut. He didn't like mowing, himself, and he thought the best house to have would be one with no lawn at all.

The house itself was larger than Rhodes had expected, though he didn't know why, exactly. It had two stories, and the roof was shingled with cedar shakes. The exterior was Austin stone, and there was a high wooden fence enclosing the back yard. There was a wide sidewalk leading up to the broad covered porch. It was easily the largest house in the addition. Rhodes figured that Miss Bobbit probably didn't have to worry about mowing her own yard.

Rhodes parked at the end of the walk and got out of the county car. There was a light burning on the ground floor, so he supposed that Miss Bobbit was at home. He could smell wood smoke. It was going to be a cold night, and someone already had a fire going.

He went up to the front door, which was really two doors, painted white. There was a doorbell on the right-hand wall, a soft light glowing behind its plastic button. Rhodes pushed the button and heard a gentle chiming in the house.

He waited for a few seconds and then the porch light came on. When the door swung open, Miss Bobbit was facing him. She hadn't changed much from the last time he had seen her, except that she looked a little older.

She must have been about forty, he guessed, though he wasn't much good at estimating the ages of women. She had a round face and a slight double chin, and her brown eyes glittered at him from behind thick glasses. The glitter might have been tears, or it might simply have been the porch light. Her mousy hair was pulled into a tight bun at the back of her head. She was not tall, not more than five-one or -two, and she was wearing some kind of long blue velour robe that reached from her shoulders to the floor and covered most of her neck as well. There was a zipper down the front.

"Sheriff Rhodes," she said. Her voice was dry. No tears there. "It's about time you got here."

Rhodes didn't see any point in pursuing that line of talk. "Can I come in?" he said.

Miss Bobbit stepped back and Rhodes walked past her into the hallway. She closed the door and led him into the living room, a place which surprised Rhodes because of the expensive furnishings, though the outside of the house should have prepared him.

The beige carpet was deep and supported by a thick pad. The couch and the two chairs probably cost more than Rhodes made in six months, and the forty-inch stereo television set hadn't come cheap. "Beauty and the Beast" was on, but the sound was muted. There was a stone fireplace that took up most of one wall, and there were logs burning behind a glass fire screen.

Miss Bobbit did not invite Rhodes to sit down. Instead, she started to lecture him.

"I want you to find Maurice Kennedy, arrest him, and put him in jail at once," she said. "He killed my father, and I will not tolerate the thought of him running around free and easy while my father is getting measured for a coffin."

"Just a minute," Rhodes said. "We don't know if Mr. Kennedy killed anyone. What gives you that idea?"

"He ran away, didn't he? Mr. Patterson made it clear that there was some kind of difficulty between Mr. Kennedy and my father, something about the stolen teeth. I want that man arrested and sent to prison."

"We don't know for sure about the teeth, either," Rhodes said.

"Well, I never! It's as plain as the nose on your face, and you don't even seem concerned. I must say, Sheriff, you don't seem to have the interests of the voters at heart."

"I'm checking into everything," Rhodes said. "For example, right now I'm checking on everyone who was seen in your father's room today." That was a pretty big exaggeration, considering that Earlene didn't even know who had been in the nursing home, much less where the four people she had seen had been going. But Rhodes didn't feel like explaining.

"What do you mean? Do you mean that you consider me a suspect in my father's death simply because I paid him a visit? Sheriff, I'll have you know that I loved my father. I'm the one who found him when he strayed away a few years ago, if you'll remember."

It was the Houston police who'd found him, but Rhodes didn't interrupt to remind her of that.

"If I left things up to you," she continued, "I'd never have seen him again. Frankly, Sheriff, I don't think you know very much about your job."

Rhodes felt awkward standing in the middle of the living room. Over Miss Bobbit's shoulder he could see Vincent running through what looked like a giant sewer pipe, his cape streaming out behind him.

"I do my best," he said. "Why don't you tell me about your visit with your father today."

Miss Bobbit's shoulders slumped in the robe, making her look even shorter. "What about it?"

"Tell me what you talked about, whether he said anything that might give us a clue as to who would want to kill him."

"He talked about his teeth, what do you think he talked about? Mr. Patterson told me that you saw him earlier this morning. What did he talk to you about?"

"His teeth," Rhodes admitted.

"That's all he talked about for the last two days, ever since Maurice Kennedy stole them. He was obsessed with those teeth."

"Was there any connection between Kennedy and your father besides the teeth?" Rhodes asked.

Miss Bobbit squared her shoulders and looked Rhodes in the eye. "What's that supposed to mean?"

"I've heard that they knew one another a long time back," Rhodes said.

"It's just like those people out there to start stories like that." Miss Bobbit waggled a finger at Rhodes. "Malicious stories started by people who don't have anything better to talk about. There's not a word of truth in any one of them."

She put her hand down by her side. "Well, I take that back. There might be some truth in what they say about Maurice Kennedy, but not about my father."

Rhodes could see that he wasn't going to get anywhere with that line of questioning. Miss Bobbit was obviously fiercely protective of her father, even though the old man was dead.

"About this afternoon," Rhodes said. "What time did you go for the visit?"

"It was about two o'clock. There was no one else there, if that's what you mean. My father could afford a private room."

"I was wondering about that," Rhodes said, looking around the living room.

"He had a little bit of gas money," Miss Bobbit said.

"Oh," Rhodes said. There were several people in Clear-view, more than you'd think, who "had a little bit of gas money," thanks to the wells that had been drilled on land to the south and east of town in the past few years.

He asked Miss Bobbit a few more questions, but he didn't learn any more. She had not stayed long, she said, because she had to go grocery shopping. Besides, she visited her father every day.

"I feel an obligation," she told Rhodes. "After all, he's . . . he *was* . . . my father. And I demand that you find the man who killed him."

"I'll do my best," Rhodes said.

Miss Bobbit looked at him from behind the thick lenses. "I hope so," she told him.

C H A P T E R

SEVEN

When he got back outside, Rhodes took a deep breath of the cold night air. Maybe it was the pressure of the lawsuit, but he was letting things get to him more than he usually did.

The murder of Mr. Bobbit, for one thing. The old man probably wouldn't have lived much longer anyway, and it seemed especially unfair for someone to rob him of the short time he had left. Despite the appearance of many of the old people in Sunny Dale, Rhodes was positive that there wasn't a one of them who would have willingly shortened his or her life.

He has said something along those lines to Mr. Stuart once, though he couldn't remember exactly what. He could remember Mr. Stuart's answer, however.

"Sheriff," Mr. Stuart had said, "you're a youngster yet, and you prob'ly still think you're gonna live forever."

Rhodes didn't feel that way at all, and he hadn't felt young for a long time, but he didn't tell Mr. Stuart that.

"Well, you won't live forever, no matter what you think," Mr. Stuart continued. "And when you get to be my age, you damn well know it. But that don't make any difference. No matter how close you are to dyin', you still think about livin'. I'm not a bit more ready to go than I was seventy-five years ago, and don't you forget it."

Rhodes hadn't forgotten, which made him doubly determined to find out who had cut short whatever time Mr. Bobbit had left.

Rhodes didn't think he was going to like dealing with Miss Bobbit, either. As he walked to the car, he told himself to be sure to find out about Mr. Bobbit's will. It might be a good idea to see who is going to get all that gas money.

It might be a good idea for him to go over to Ivy Daniel's house, too. He had told her that he would come by. He hadn't known about the murder at the time, however, and he was going to be late.

Still, he could see Ivy and continue the investigation at the same time. She wouldn't mind a trip to the courthouse. At least he didn't think she would.

He was hungry, too. He would stop by his house and get something for them to eat. He had made pimiento cheese yesterday, and there was still plenty left for some sandwiches.

He parked in the driveway beside the house and went into the back yard to feed Speedo, sort of a border collie whose real name was Mr. Earl. Speedo ran to meet him, barking and jumping. He roughhoused with the dog a little, then gave him some water and a bowl full of Ol' Roy. He thought it would be nice to have as few troubles as Speedo did. Dogs didn't have to worry much about nursing homes.

He went inside and checked the refrigerator. The pimiento cheese looked fine. The secret was to make it with American cheese, not cheddar, and to use real salad dressing, not the "light" kind or the kind with no cholesterol. He felt a little guilty about that, but there was always the exercise bike. Besides, he was using oat bran bread. Maybe things would sort of balance out.

The bread was a little dry, but Rhodes made four sandwiches and put them in plastic bags. He didn't have any drinks to take, but they could get a Dr Pepper at the courthouse. He put the bagged sandwiches in a paper sack and stuck in a couple of napkins.

Speedo wanted to play some more, but Rhodes didn't have time. He tossed the sack of sandwiches in the front seat and left.

As he drove to Ivy's house, he wondered just where they would be living after they got married. It was something he had thought of before, but no decision had been made. He'd just naturally assumed that they would move to his place, but what if Ivy had the same idea about *her* place? Just thinking about it made Rhodes uncomfortable, and he put it out of his mind.

When Ivy answered his knock at her door, she appeared glad to see him.

"I was thinking you might have gotten involved in something," she said. She had short, curly hair with a little gray in it, but her face was still smooth and unlined. Rhodes still found it hard to believe that he was actually going to marry her.

"I did get involved," he said. "But I thought you might like to give me a little help." He knew that she would. She liked helping out with his law enforcement duties when she could.

"Will we need the siren?" she asked. That was another thing she liked.

"Not this time," Rhodes said. "We're just going to be doing a little research."

"What kind of research?"

He told her about Mr. Bobbit's murder, starting with the missing teeth.

"That's awful," Ivy said. "That poor old man. I suppose

65

you want to check out that story about Maurice Kennedy killing someone sixty years ago?"

"That's it," Rhodes said.

"I don't see how that could have anything to do with Mr. Bobbit. It was so long ago," Ivy said.

"It probably wouldn't seem that way to them," Rhodes said. That was something else he had learned from Mr. Stuart, and he was beginning to see nagging symptoms of it in his own life.

"You know," Mr. Stuart had said one day, "it seems like I can remember things that happened sixty or seventy years ago better than I can things that happened yesterday." He gave a little smile. "I can remember the first automobile I ever rode in, a Model T Ford. Remember the day I rode in it just as plain as anything. Summertime. Hot? Let me tell you, it was hot. My daddy was drivin'. We were ridin' down that road, all the hot dust blowin'. I still remember the way that dust smelled. But if you asked me what the weather was like last week? Hell, I couldn't tell you."

Rhodes understood what the old man meant. It was getting a lot easier for him to recall the details of a movie he'd seen twenty years before than of one he'd seen last month.

"What about supper?" Ivy said, getting his mind back on the track. "Have you eaten?"

"I brought us something," Rhodes told her.

"What?"

"It's a surprise," he said.

"Let me get my coat," she said. "I can't resist a surprise."

The courthouse was closed and locked, but Rhodes had a key. They went inside and walked across the marble floor, their steps echoing hollowly down the hall.

66

Ivy took Rhodes's arm. "It seems a lot different in here at night."

"Sure does." Rhodes didn't say so, but he liked the courthouse even better at night, when it was entirely empty. The building was not quite as old as the jail, and it had been kept up better, but it was still a reminder of the past, of the history of the county and all the things that had happened there. Rhodes felt closer to that history when he was practically the only one in the building.

They went up the stairs to Rhodes's office. Ivy had never been inside before.

"This isn't bad," she said, looking around as he turned on the light.

Rhodes put the sack of sandwiches on the desk. "How about a Dr Pepper?" he said.

"Sounds good," Ivy said, and Rhodes went to get the drinks.

When he came back, she was looking at the shelves on the right wall. There were bound volumes of old records there, and she was looking for the ones from sixty years ago.

"Could be fifty-nine years," Rhodes said, setting the bottles on the desk. "Or sixty-one. Or anywhere in that area."

"We may as well try sixty-five years first, then work forward," Ivy said, pulling down the thick volume. The top of it was covered with dust. "Don't you ever clean in here?" She blew on the dust, which came off the top of the volume in a cloud.

"Somebody comes in and sweeps out, I guess," Rhodes said. "Empties the trash can." He looked under the desk. Sure enough, Parry's cigar was gone. "I don't think they do much dusting."

Ivy brought the book over to the desk and plunked it down. Dust came out of the binding and puffed up around it.

"I hope you clean better than that at home," Ivy said.

Rhodes didn't want to talk about that. He opened the sack and brought out the sandwiches. "Pimiento cheese," he said.

"My favorite," Ivy said.

He couldn't tell if she was kidding him or not. He handed her a sandwich, and she opened the plastic bag. He gave her a napkin.

"All the comforts," she said.

Rhodes pulled the chair that Jack Parry had sat in earlier around to the other side of the desk so that they could both look at the records as they ate. He began flipping through the pages while Ivy took a bite from her sandwich.

The old records made interesting reading because the twenties had really roared in Clearview; in fact, the town had been much larger than it now was, thanks to the discovery of oil. People had poured in from all over the state, all over the nation, really, to try cashing in on the boom times. The population of the town had swelled to four or five times its usual size in a matter of weeks after the first well was brought in, and there was a consequent increase in crime.

The sheriff for most of those years had been a man named Reb Trotter, just as Mr. Stuart had said, and Rhodes didn't envy him. He'd had to deal with more barroom fights, burglaries, robberies, and murder in just one year than Rhodes had ever encountered, and at the same time there were the same kinds of recurring petty problems that Rhodes was still dealing with today, including stray dogs, marital spats, and kids throwing rocks.

"I didn't realize that people called the sheriff about things like this," Ivy said, reading over one of the reports on a dog digging in a woman's flower bed.

"You'd be surprised at some of the calls we public

68

servants get," Rhodes said, turning the pages and looking for Maurice Kennedy's name. "How's the sandwich?"

"Great," Ivy said, taking another bite.

Rhodes took a bite of his own sandwich. It wasn't bad.

It took them a while to find what they were looking for. The sandwiches were long gone, and to Rhodes's regret he had eaten three of them. He'd intended to share them equally with Ivy, but she had insisted that she wanted only one.

The report with the information he wanted was from sixty-one years previously, right at the end of the boom days. Mrs. Stuart had remembered the story quite accurately, which was no surprise to Rhodes, though she had not given him all the details, not having been an actual participant in the events.

She had not described the fight at the dance, for example. According to the witnesses Reb Trotter had questioned, Maurice Kennedy and Louis Horn had gotten into an argument about who was going to take Peggy Rainey home. There had been some shouting and pushing inside the hall, and then the argument had moved outside and turned ugly. Horn and Kennedy had started slugging one another, but no one seemed quite sure who had gotten in the first lick, either that or no one wanted to say.

Some of the other men had managed to break up the fight, and Kennedy and Horn had gone to their cars and left, Horn alone and Kennedy with a friend. It had been thundering and lightning throughout the fight, and the witnesses said that as the men were driving away the rain started coming down in sheets. Everyone either got into his own car and left or ran back inside the hall, and no one saw whether Horn and Kennedy went their separate ways or whether one car followed the other.

The only thing that was certain was that Horn never

went home that night, and the next day Horn's Model A was found parked down by the river that ran through the county about five miles north of Clearview. The car appeared to have gotten stuck, and there were some signs that another car had been there, but the heavy rain had wiped out any really useful clues, like tire tracks.

The rain had begun far to the west and swept all across the state, causing the river to flood. It was running out of its banks, and it was running more swiftly than it normally did, though it didn't seem to Trotter to have been too wide or too swift for a sober man who was a good swimmer to drown in. No one at the dance had seen Horn drinking, and he'd seemed plenty sober during his fight with Kennedy. And Horn was well known to be a good swimmer.

Despite the latter fact, most people seemed to think that Horn had gotten stuck, wandered off in the wrong direction, and fallen in the river, where he'd probably drowned.

If that was the case, however, his body should have turned up somewhere down the river, or at least Sheriff Trotter thought so.

It never did.

It could have caught up on a log that drifted to shore and been hidden along the bank, or it could have been dragged under by roots and vines and never come up, but that didn't seem likely. Sheriff Trotter had gotten a search party together and looked along both banks for miles without success. He'd had the river dragged, with the same lack of result.

And of course he'd questioned a lot of people, because he had reason to suspect that there might be more to Horn's death than a simple drowning.

There had been the fight for one thing, along with Kennedy's reputation as a hellraiser. Kennedy had already been in serious trouble because of another fight over a woman; in that one he had gouged out a man's eye. Rhodes had seen that report in a volume from two years earlier.

70

Trotter had not been able to prove a thing against Kennedy in the Horn case, however. No one had seen Kennedy after the dance, but he said that he had gone straight to his house after taking his friend home. There was no proof that his car had been near the river. It had been washed clean, but Kennedy said he always liked to clean his car after a big rain. Kennedy was bruised up, but he attributed that to his earlier fight at the dance. The friend he had left the dance with backed him up a hundred percent on every point.

There were two other things that Mrs. Stuart had not mentioned, probably because she had not known about them.

One was that one of the witnesses interviewed by Sheriff Trotter was a man named Andrew West.

The other was that the friend who had left the dance with Kennedy was a man named Lloyd Bobbit. It appeared that there was indeed a connection between the two men, in spite of what Miss Bobbit had said.

Somehow, Rhodes was not surprised.

"I guess there isn't much doubt it's the same man," Ivy said. She was leaning back in the chair looking at the ceiling.

"Not much," Rhodes said. "Lloyd Bobbit isn't exactly a common name, and the Stuarts told me the two of them were friends in those days."

Ivy had a faraway look in her eyes. "It's kind of a shame when you think about it," she said.

"It's worse than a shame," Rhodes said.

"I don't mean Louis Horn," Ivy said. "It's more than that."

"What is it, then?"

"Thinking about those old men, living out there in Sunny Dale. Nothing to do but watch television and play

71

checkers. Their lives are just about played out. But sixty years ago they were energetic and spirited, going to dances, arguing about young girls, having fights . . ."

It was too close to what Rhodes had been thinking that morning for comfort.

"How about some dessert?" he said, closing the volume of records and standing up.

"You brought dessert, too?"

"I didn't bring anything, but I can get us something. What would you like?"

"What choice do I have?"

"Not much," Rhodes admitted. He tried to think what might be in the machine. "Probably just some kind of cookies."

"Surprise me," Ivy said.

Rhodes went out and came back with a package of chocolate cookies with cream filling.

"There's something else we need to talk about," he said as he tore open the package.

"Yes," Ivy said. "Getting married."

Rhodes ripped the cellophane more than he had intended and the cookies tumbled out onto the desk. He started picking them up.

"I didn't mean that," he said. He gave her a cookie and sat down. Then he told her about the lawsuit.

She didn't take the news as well as Rhodes had thought she would, and she didn't see anything funny about the million dollars.

"This isn't going to interfere with the wedding, is it?" she said.

"I don't think so," Rhodes said. "It's just that a lot of things are happening at the same time."

"I wouldn't want anything to interfere with the wedding." Ivy had a steely look in her eye. Rhodes wondered if she suspected that anything was wrong. Not that it was.

"Nothing's going to interfere," he said. "I just wanted

you to know about the lawsuit. There's going to be a lot of talk."

"You didn't do anything wrong."

"No. But that won't stop people from talking." Rhodes looked at his watch. It was after eleven o'clock. They'd spent longer looking over the records than he'd thought. "We'd better be getting on home," he said.

"That's something we need to talk about," Ivy said. "Where home is going to be."

Rhodes didn't want to get into that now, but he thought he might as well. "Wherever you want it to be," he said.

He wondered how it would be, living in her house, which must have contained a lot of memories of her late husband, just as his house contained memories of his wife. The memories were something they would both have to deal with.

Ivy smiled. "I was going to say the same thing. I guess it doesn't really matter, does it, as long as we're together."

"No," Rhodes said, smiling. "It doesn't matter a bit."

After he and Ivy left the courthouse, Rhodes thought it would be a good idea for him to go by the jail, check in with Hack, and see what was going on. Friday night was usually pretty lively.

A truck had jackknifed out on the highway, someone had stolen a street sign near downtown, a woman had locked her keys in the car in the Wal-Mart parking lot, and a drunk had been picked up wandering around a residential neighborhood, but that was all. Nothing unusual, and nothing calling for a personal visit from the sheriff.

Rhodes took Ivy home and they watched part of the late movie, something called *Singing Guns*, with Vaughn Monroe.

"I thought he was a bandleader," Ivy said. "'Racing with the Moon.'"

"That's him," Rhodes said. "He doesn't look too bad as a cowboy, though."

Ivy didn't agree. She thought he was too beefy.

"What have you got against beefy?" Rhodes said, thinking about those three sandwiches.

"Nothing," Ivy said. "I just think cowboys ought to be slimmer, like Roy Rogers."

"Oh," Rhodes said, vowing to get back to the stationary bike as soon as he got a chance.

CHAPTER

EIGHT

The next morning Rhodes went by the jail to see if anyone had reported finding Maurice Kennedy. No one had. He told Hack to find out if Bobbit had had a lawyer, and if so to call and ask about a will.

Then he drove out the Obert Road to talk to Andy West, whose father had been interviewed by Sheriff Reb Trotter sixty-one years before.

The Obert Road led, naturally enough, to the town of Obert, which hardly existed anymore. There had once been a college there, and most of the buildings still remained, sitting high atop Obert's Hill and overlooking the valley below. The last classes there had been taught around the time of the end of the oil boom. Some hotshot regional publisher and rare-book dealer from Houston had bought the buildings and grounds from whoever had owned them last and was beginning to restore them. He had the idea of making some kind of museum and library out of them.

Rhodes could not see the college buildings from Andy West's filling station. What was left of the town of Obert was around a sweeping curve and up the hill.

Filling station didn't really describe West's place of

75

business. It was one of those establishments that tried to capitalize on fake and grating rusticity that the owner laid on by the truckload. Starting about a mile down the road there were signs proclaiming that travelers were approaching THE KOUNTRY STOAR where there were BARGINS GALORE! Not to mention such items as ICE CREEM, ICE KOLD DRINKS, GARDIN SUPPLYS, and FRESH VEJTIBLES.

Rhodes decided not to hold West entirely responsible for the signs, however. The paint was old and peeling, and they might very well have been put there by West's father.

The store itself was a rambling and ramshackle affair covered with peeling white paint. Rusted screens leaned out of windows, and the roof needed new shingles. There was a parking area covered with pea gravel and a covered walkway had been built out over the drive so that no one would have to stand in the rain to get gas from the three pumps that stood in front of the store. The pumps were fairly new, certainly the newest thing there. Rhodes didn't know whether that was because West wanted the store to look authentically old and rustic or whether because about the only business he did was selling gas.

Rhodes parked the car and got out. There were no other cars there, which wasn't much of a surprise. The Obert Road was not exactly a main highway.

He crunched across the gravel to the front door. There were two rusted metal lawn chairs sitting beside the entrance, but there was no one in them. It was too cold to be sitting outside.

There was a cowbell tied to the doorknob with a leather thong. It jangled when Rhodes pushed open the door, and it jangled again when the door swung shut behind him.

The inside of the store was dimly lit with a few fluorescent bulbs hanging high up near the ceiling. There wasn't much to see. The wooden shelves were sparsely lined with dusty canned goods, cereal cartons, and jelly jars. Rhodes didn't see any sign of "gardin supplys."

He didn't see any sign of the proprietor, either, so he kept on walking to the back of the store, where there was a white refrigerated meat cooler with a glass front. There were only a few cuts of meat visible inside, some rump roasts and T-bones, along with a large piece of cheddar cheese. Apparently West's business was not prospering.

There was a man bent over behind the cooler, putting one-gallon plastic milk containers inside. When he finished, he stood up and looked at Rhodes.

"Can I help you, Sheriff?" he said, noting the badge and pistol on Rhodes's belt.

He was short and burly, with wide shoulders and a solid midsection that caused a bulge in the middle of the full-length white apron he was wearing. His short black hair was cut in a bristly buzz, and he had thick black eyebrows that grew straight across his forehead with no gap.

"I'd like to talk to you for a minute," Rhodes said. "If you're Andy West, that is."

"That's me." West dried his hands on his apron. "What about?"

"About your father. Is he in Sunny Dale?"

"That's right. He had a stroke a while back. Still partially paralyzed. He hasn't done anything wrong, has he?"

"I don't think so," Rhodes said. "But there was a man killed there yesterday."

"I heard about that," West said. "Mr. Bobbit."

"When did you hear that?"

"Brenda called me. Brenda Bobbit. His daughter."

Rhodes was interested. Why would Miss Bobbit be calling Andy West? He asked West, and the answer was a surprise.

"We've been going out a little," West said. "We met one time when I was with my daddy there at the nursing home, and we got to talking. We both had our parents in there, and one thing kind of led to another."

"Your father knew another man in Sunny Dale," Rhodes said. "Maurice Kennedy."

"I think I've met Mr. Kennedy," West said. "He's pretty spry for a man his age."

"He must be," Rhodes said. "He seems to have disappeared."

West had heard about that, too. "Brenda thinks he killed her daddy," he said. "Stole his teeth, and then killed him. He was a rough old cob, back in his younger days."

"Did your father ever talk about those days?"

"Ever' now and then. He said Mr. Kennedy killed a man."

"Nobody ever proved that," Rhodes said. "Did your father say how he knew?"

"Nope. He told it for the truth, though. They got in a fight at a dance, and Kennedy killed him."

"Were you there yesterday, at Sunny Dale?"

"I went by to see my daddy for a while. Didn't stay long. Didn't hear about Mr. Bobbit, though."

Rhodes talked to West for a while longer, then left. The man didn't have much to say, but that didn't bother Rhodes. His way of solving crimes was based on a very unscientific method that had nothing to do with computers. He talked to people, formed opinions, trusted his judgments, and tried to figure out who was lying to him. Sooner or later it usually worked out; he just had to keep talking, whether the people he talked to had anything to say or not. He had a lot more people to talk to about Mr. Bobbit, a lot more questions to ask.

His next stop was Sunny Dale. He wanted to get addresses for Lyle Everett and Dave Foley, but he also wanted to talk to the elder Mr. West and to the Stuarts.

From the latter two he learned that Maurice Kennedy was not the most popular resident of Sunny Dale.

"Didn't belong here, if you ask me," Mr. Stuart said. "He never did want to talk to you or have anything to do with anybody. I think he just lived here because it was easy for him and he could cause trouble for the rest of us."

Mr. Patterson confirmed Mr. Stuart's suspicions. "He didn't really belong here," he said. "He sold his home and moved in here because he got tired of keeping house for himself. And because he was lonely, I think. Most of the people his age were either in bad health or in a home, so he didn't have any friends. Not that he had many friends here, either."

Rhodes asked about the friends.

"He talked to Mr. Bobbit some, I think. But mostly people avoided him. He was always complaining about one thing or another. Either the food was too bland, or it was too hot in his room, or there was dust under his bed, or someone had thrown away his newspaper before he finished reading it."

"He was a troublemaker, then?" They were in Patterson's office, and Rhodes was sitting in the chair without a cushion. It wasn't any more comfortable than it had been the day before.

"Not a troublemaker, exactly. Dealing with old people, you have to expect a few complaints. They like for things to go their way, and you can't really blame them."

"But he complained more than the others?"

"Yes. But it really wasn't so bad. I can't understand why he would run off. He wasn't *that* unhappy here."

"What if he killed Mr. Bobbit?"

"That would explain it. I guess," Mr. Patterson said.

"What about Mr. West?" Rhodes asked. "Was he one of Kennedy's friends?"

Mr. Patterson steepled his fingers and looked pious. "Mr. West doesn't really have many friends, poor man. He had a stroke, you know."

Rhodes wondered what difference that made.

"Conversation with him isn't always pleasant," Patterson explained. "It's not what he says," he added. "His mind is still very sharp. But, well, his speech is a little slurred and he looks a little . . . well, like. . . ." Patterson let the words trail off, unable to say just how Mr. West looked.

"Like he had a stroke?" Rhodes said.

"That's it. That's it exactly. Like he had a stroke. Probably some of our guests here don't like to be reminded so acutely that it could happen to them, too."

"To any of us," Rhodes said.

"Yes, well, some are more susceptible than others. Age can be a factor." Patterson smoothed his hair, which did not need smoothing. "I suppose you haven't found Mr. Kennedy yet?"

"No," Rhodes said. "I don't think he could get very far, though, without a car, and we haven't had any stolen vehicles reported. He didn't have one of his own, did he?"

"No," Patterson said. "He didn't. He was perfectly capable of driving, however. His eyesight and reflexes were excellent for a man his age."

Rhodes thought for a second about his own eyesight. "And he didn't have any friends in the community that he could stay with?"

"I don't believe that he did. As I mentioned, I suspect that one of the reasons he came here was loneliness."

Rhodes couldn't imagine where Kennedy had gotten to. It had been cold last night, getting down near freezing. Where could a man nearly ninety spend the night if he didn't have a friend to give him a room or a car to drive somewhere in? He hoped the deputies had checked the motels. He would have to make sure they did.

"I don't suppose that anyone saw him leave," Rhodes said.

Patterson shook his head. "I'm afraid not. He just slipped away. We don't keep prisoners here, you know. The doors aren't locked."

"I know," Rhodes said. But he still wouldn't want to live there.

It turned out that Andrew West, Sr., had a room right next door to the one in which Mr. Bobbit had died. West was lying on his bed, watching television.

At least Rhodes thought that was what he was doing. It was hard to tell, because of the odd angle of the old man's head. He had the head of his bed elevated, and his body was facing the TV set that was on a shelf fixed to the wall of the room, but his head was twisted to the right, his chin practically resting on his right shoulder. His mouth hung slightly open, and there was a towel pinned to the shoulder of his pajamas. There was a damp stain on the towel.

There was a fishing show on TV. Two men were in a bass boat, casting spinner baits in and around some lily pads. The lake looked mighty fishy to Rhodes, and he wished that he was one of the men in the boat.

Rhodes tapped on the door frame. "Can I come in?" he said.

The man in the bed said something that sounded roughly like "Nobody's stopping you," and Rhodes entered the room.

There was a chair by the bed, and Rhodes sat down. "Watching TV?" he said.

"Hell, no, I'm playing pocket pool. What the hell does it look like I'm doing?" West's speech was slurred, as Patterson had said, but Rhodes had no difficulty understanding him. He felt a little silly about his question.

"I'm Sheriff Dan Rhodes," Rhodes said. "I was wondering if I could talk to you for a minute."

"You're doing it ain't you?"

"I guess I am," Rhodes said.

On the TV one of the men got a hard strike. He reared back on his rod, setting the hook solidly, and the fish began

81

to make a run for the vegetation, the line cutting through the water and the drag on the reel singing.

"You fish?" West said.

"Not often enough," Rhodes told him, watching wistfully as the man on TV lipped and boated a bass that looked like it would go a solid five pounds. The spinner bait with a yellow-and-black rubber skirt dangled from the fish's jaw.

West fumbled around on the covers with his right hand and found the remote control. He pushed a button and the TV snapped off.

"I used to go fishing," he said. "Had me a little Skeeter bass boat, place on the lake. I was out on that water all the time." His voice was virtually toneless, but Rhodes could feel the emotion in it. "I don't go much anymore," he said.

Rhodes couldn't think of anything to say to that. He sat there for a minute, looking at the blank screen of the TV.

"Didn't mean to cheer you up so much," West said. "I bet you didn't come in here to talk about fishing."

"No," Rhodes said. "I didn't." He told him what he had come in there to talk about.

"Yep, my boy came to see me yesterday," Mr. West said. "Sat right in that chair till I woke up from my nap. He has to get somebody to watch the store when he comes in, but he does it two or three times a week, you can count on that."

Rhodes asked about the night Louis Horn died.

"I remember that night about as well as anything," West said. "Ain't no doubt in my mind that Maurice Kennedy killed that Horn boy. Not a doubt in my mind."

"Do you think he killed Mr. Bobbit?" Rhodes asked.

It was hard to read West's face. It was lined and wrinkled, and he hadn't been shaved yet that day. The partial paralysis didn't help, either. But Rhodes could have sworn that something changed in the old man's faded brown eyes. He looked somehow more cunning, secretive.

"He did it, all right."

"How do you know? Did you see him? Did you hear anything?"

"I didn't see him, but he did it all right."

Rhodes sighed inwardly. West had no proof, had seen nothing either time, but he was sure Kennedy was guilty of two murders. That was often the way it was. People were convinced of the guilt or innocence of others, but they had no evidence at all to back up their convictions. And they wondered why the sheriff didn't rush out and make an arrest.

But there had been that change in West's eyes.

"Why are you so sure?" Rhodes said.

"Because Bobbit had the goods on him," West said. "And he was going to tell the world."

"What was he going to tell?"

"He knew where Kennedy dumped Horn's body," West said. "That's what he was going to tell."

Rhodes pulled his chair a little closer to the bed. "Are you sure about that?"

"Damn right, I'm sure. I heard 'em talking about it." West tried to hitch himself up a little higher in the bed. "People think I'm just a piece of furniture, think I don't know what's going on, but I do. I maybe can't run a damn race or drive a car, but there's nothing wrong with my ears."

"You heard Bobbit tell Kennedy he was going to say something about a body?"

"Which word didn't you understand? 'Course I heard him."

"When?" Rhodes said.

"Yesterday morning. They were arguing in Bobbit's room. It's right next door, in case you didn't notice."

Rhodes had noticed. "What did they say, exactly?"

"Well, now that's not so easy. Bobbit didn't always make a lot of sense; it was like he sort of faded in and out."

Having talked to Bobbit, Rhodes knew what West meant. "Just do the best you can, then."

"They were arguing about teeth," West said. "Bobbit said that Kennedy had stole his teeth, and Kennedy said what if he did? What was Bobbit gonna do about it? And Bobbit said something like he knew where the bodies were buried."

"That's a pretty common expression," Rhodes said.

"Yep. He didn't say it like that, maybe. More like, he knew where the body was *dumped*, like I said before."

"I don't guess he said where."

"Oh, yeah. He even said that. Said it was dumped down a well."

Rhodes didn't say anything for a minute. He'd had a recent experience with looking for a body in a well; it wasn't something that had turned out the way he'd thought it would, and he wasn't eager to repeat it.

Then he said, "Did he mention where the well was located?"

"Nope, didn't say that. Kennedy didn't give him a chance. Just said that if Bobbit tried to tell, wouldn't anybody believe him because he was a senile old fart. Then he left."

"Kennedy?"

"Yep. Walked out of the room and down the hall. I saw him go by, but he didn't look in here."

"Did you tell your son any of this?"

"Nope, but I've told him about Kennedy before. I knew all along that he killed that Horn boy."

"Why didn't you say anything to Mr. Patterson about this yesterday?"

"Nobody asked me. Like I said, they think I'm just a piece of the furniture. But I can still do a lot of things if I get the chance."

Rhodes wished he had talked to West earlier. "Did you

see anybody else go into Bobbit's room? His daughter? A man named Lyle Everett or one named Dave Foley?"

"Nope. Don't even know those men. I think their mamas are in here, though. I've heard the names."

"And you didn't hear anything when Mr. Bobbit was killed?"

"Musta been taking my nap," West said. I sleep pretty hard, don't hear much. These doors and walls are pretty thick."

"I thought the doors were always kept open," Rhodes said.

"Usually are, but you can shut 'em if you want to. Long as they don't stay shut too long, nobody'll say anything."

Rhodes talked for a few minutes more, but West was obviously tiring. As Rhodes left, the old man switched the TV set back on, but the fishing show was over.

Rhodes went back to Patterson's office. "I want to search Kennedy's room now. Has anyone been in there yet?"

"No," Patterson said. "I've kept it locked."

Rhodes didn't know what he hoped to find. False teeth, maybe, or some clue to Kennedy's whereabouts.

He found neither. The room was practically bare. There were five shirts hanging in the closet, a run-down pair of Hushpuppies on the closet floor, and two pairs of Levi's Gentleman's Jeans. There was a kit of toilet articles in a drawer of the nightstand. That was all.

"He didn't have many personal possessions," Patterson said. "Not very many of our guests do. When you get to be their age, you know that material things don't matter very much."

"I wonder why he left his toothbrush and razor," Rhodes said.

Patterson frowned. "Maybe he was in a hurry," he said.

A big hurry, Rhodes thought. The kind of hurry you might be in if you'd just killed a man.

CHAPTER

NINE

The wind had picked up out of the north and seemed to cut right through Rhodes's corduroy jacket. The wind had brought clouds with it, thin and gray and high. The sun was a dim white ball.

Rhodes went back to the jail to see if Hack had found out about Mr. Bobbit's lawyer, though it seemed more and more likely that Maurice Kennedy was the guilty party. Now all they had to do was find him.

Ruth Grady was there when Rhodes got in, and she told him that Kennedy had done a really good job of disappearing. "He's not registered at any of the motels under his own name, and I described him to all the clerks. They don't have anyone like that staying with them."

Checking the motels was a fairly easy job in Clearview. There was only one establishment that anyone with a family would consider stopping in, and three of a somewhat sleazier variety.

"There are probably a couple of vacant houses close to Sunny Dale," Rhodes suggested. "He might have broken in and stayed there."

"I've already looked," Ruth said. "He's not in any of them. I checked all around on the county roads, too."

She was the only deputy Rhodes had who had actually studied law enforcement, and she was sometimes a step ahead of him. Hack and Lawton had resented her at first, simply because she was a woman, but they had soon come to realize that she was a top-notch deputy. Rhodes had known it all along, and she had gotten him out of tough situations more than once.

"How about those state boys with their computers?" Rhodes asked Hack, who had to admit that the Department of Public Safety, even with its technological superiority, had not yet called in with any leads to Kennedy's whereabouts.

"I don't see how a man, especially a man that old, could disappear like that," Ruth said. "Where could he go?"

"He ain't all that old," Hack said.

"Sorry," Ruth said. "I didn't mean to imply anything. But it's hard for anybody to disappear so quickly, much less someone who can't get around very fast."

"Who said he couldn't get around fast? Just because he's old don't mean he can't get around."

Ruth knew when to cut her losses. She changed the subject. "Any other suspects, Sheriff?"

"Nobody solid. What about Mr. Bobbit's will, Hack?"

Hack got a pitiful look on his face and put on a quavery voice. "What're you askin' me for? I'm so old and feeble, I can't hardly get around to findin' out things like that."

"Never mind the old and feeble act. We all know better. What about it?"

Hack grinned to show that there were no hard feelings. "His lawyer's Tom Dunstable. He wouldn't say anything about the will, though."

Rhodes hadn't expected him to. "I'll talk to him later." He gave Ruth the paper with the names of Everett and Foley on it. "See what you can find out about those two.

And if you get a chance, check with the dentists to see who made Bobbit's teeth. See if they could be worn by someone else. I'll put Buddy to looking for Kennedy. He can't have gotten too far."

"Right," Hack said. "Bein' as how he's so old and feeble."

Rhodes smiled at Ruth, secure in the knowledge that his back was to Hack, who couldn't see the smile.

Hack was about to say something else when the door opened. Pushed by the wind, it slammed back against the wall.

A young red-haired man stood in the doorway. "Sorry about that," he said. He reached for the doorknob and closed the door. He looked like a first-year college student, with freckles sprinkled across his cheeks and the bridge of his nose. He was wearing a denim jacket and jeans; his boots were snakeskin.

What bothered Rhodes was the tape recorder the young man had hanging from a strap around his neck.

"I'm Larry Redden," he said. He had a deep, clear voice that made him sound twenty years older than he appeared to be. He looked at Rhodes. "Are you the sheriff?"

Rhodes admitted that he was. He introduced Hack and Ruth.

"I'm from the radio station," Redden said. He didn't have to say which one. There was only one station in Clearview. "You've probably heard me on the air."

No one had heard of him, but no one wanted to say so.

He noticed the blank looks and laughed. "Oh. I guess I should have said that my air name's Red Rogers."

Rhodes knew that name. Red Rogers did a five-hour country music show in the mornings. He also did all the morning newscasts and an hour-long local news show at noon. On that one he talked about "All the news of special interest to *you*, the citizens of Clearview." Rhodes liked the tape recorder less and less.

"I've heard your show," Rhodes said.

"I'm here to interview you about the lawsuit that a former prisoner has filed against you and the county, Sheriff Rhodes," Redden, or Rogers, said. "Is there a place where we can sit down?"

"I don't think I ought to be giving any interviews," Rhodes said. "The lawsuit will be tried in the courts, not on the radio."

"But our listeners have a right to know about conditions in the jail that their tax money supports," Redden said. "We don't have to talk about the lawsuit at all if you think we shouldn't. I'll just mention it, and then we can just talk about the leaky roof, the lack of an exercise program, neglected prisoners, things like that."

"No prisoner in this jail ever got neglected," Hack said. "You can tell your listeners that I said so."

"Just a second," Redden said, glad to find someone willing to talk. "Let me get this recorder set up."

He put the recorder down on Hack's desk and pushed a couple of buttons. "It's got a built-in mike," he said. Then he rewound the tape and played it. It repeated his words: "It's got a built-in mike."

"Ready to go," he said as he rewound the tape again. He looked at Hack and pushed the record buttons. "Now, what's your position here?"

"I'm the dispatcher," Hack said. As if to prove his point, the telephone rang. Hack was answering it when Rhodes sneaked out the door. Redden looked around when the wind hit him, but by then it was too late. Rhodes was already gone.

Tom Dunstable had his office in a remodeled two-bedroom house about a block from the jail. Rhodes decided to walk. He hated to leave Hack at the mercy of the radio reporter like that, but he had an idea that Red

Rogers, boy reporter, might have met his match. Rhodes's only regret was that Lawton had not been there. Maybe Red's luck would be running bad and Lawton would come in while the interview was still going on.

Rhodes certainly hoped so.

Dunstable had been a lawyer in Blacklin County since passing the bar exam more than twenty years before. Rhodes had known him ever since he was a skinny young man with a head of thick blond hair. Now he was a rotund middle-aged man with only a fringe of hair remaining. The top of his head was completely bald. He didn't get up when Rhodes came into his office.

"Too damn fat to be getting up and down all the time," he said, waving Rhodes to a seat in a plush red leather chair. The walls of his office were lined with wooden book shelves with glass fronts, and there was a computer on his desk. Rhodes had come in through the secretary's office. She had a computer, too. Hack would have been envious.

"I guess I know what you're after," Dunstable said. He was leaning back in his own posh chair with his hands clasped on his belly. "Hack called me early this morning."

"He said you didn't tell him anything about a will," Rhodes said.

"I wouldn't be telling you, if I hadn't called and talked to Miss Bobbit. She said it was all right. Besides, I don't like giving out information on the phone. You never know who you might be talking to."

"You knew it was Hack, though."

"He said that's who he was. But I figured if you really wanted to know, you'd be over here yourself."

"You were right. So what can you tell me about Lloyd Bobbit's will? Did he have a lot of money? And if he did, who's he leaving it to?"

"You're not going to like hearing this, Sheriff," Dunstable said.

"Tell me anyway."

"It's a sizable estate, all right. His daughter gets most of it." Dunstable smiled a fat smile. "I know what you're thinking. Motive. I can see it in your eyes. But you're wrong. Here's the part you aren't going to like."

Rhodes waited patiently. Sometimes it seemed like the whole world was getting like Hack and Lawton.

"The thing is," Dunstable said, "his daughter doesn't need the money."

"Everybody needs money," Rhodes said. "Even sheriffs and lawyers. Why do you say Miss Bobbit doesn't?"

"She already has it."

"Then how can he be leaving it to her?" If Hack and Lawton ever needed a third party, they could recruit Dunstable.

"Well, she doesn't *really* have it. But she has power of attorney. She was in control of the estate. Her father's death just complicates things."

That didn't make things look too good for Maurice Kennedy. Then Rhodes thought of something. "You said his daughter got *most* of it. Who gets the rest? And how much is the rest?"

Dunstable looked a little uncomfortable, as if he'd had a mid-morning snack that didn't agree with him. "There is a small amount going to another party."

"I know that," Rhodes said. "You told me, remember? What I want to know is the name of the other party. And how much he's getting. Or she."

Dunstable shifted in the chair. "It's not actually a he or a she," he said.

"Maybe you'd better explain that," Rhodes said, wondering if it were possible that Dunstable could be related to either Hack or Lawton. He didn't think so, but you never knew.

"It's a place," Dunstable said.

Maybe it was just that lawyers didn't like to give out information for free. "What place?" Rhodes said.

"Well, actually, it's the Sunny Dale Nursing Home."

Rhodes suddenly felt as if he might be getting somewhere. "Sunny Dale. And how much is the place getting?"

"In the neighborhood of a hundred thousand."

A little gas money, Rhodes thought. He wondered how much would be considered a lot.

"That's an unusual bequest, isn't it?" he said. "Does the daughter know about it?"

Dunstable smiled again. He wasn't uncomfortable with the question. "It was her idea."

"She *wanted* her father to leave that much money to Sunny Dale?"

"I think she had the idea that they'd take better care of him if they knew how much he appreciated them. Give him sort of special treatment. And she could afford it."

"What about that part of a will that talks about 'being of sound mind'?"

Dunstable stopped smiling. "Mr. Bobbit was perfectly lucid when I changed the will. His daughter was with him and would certainly vouch for his complete lucidity."

Rhodes thought about what Dunstable had told him. Then he stood up. "Well, Tom, I appreciate you telling me all this. I'm sure it'll be a help to me."

Dunstable continued to sit. "Always glad to oblige an officer of the law," he said.

Banks in small towns had changed a great deal since Rhodes was a boy. He remembered them as being a lot like the county courthouse was now, cavernous buildings with sixteen-foot marble ceilings, silent fans dangling down and stirring the air in summer. The dignified tellers, often male, stood behind their windows and silently attended the customers and checked everything on adding machines. In those days, too, no one worried about carrying his personal checkbook around with him. You could pick up a counter check in any store and cash it without even showing a driver's license.

Now you couldn't cash anything that wasn't personalized, and even at that you were lucky to get out of the store without giving a blood sample and leaving your first-born child as a hostage. He couldn't remember the last time he had seen a male teller. Banks were staffed mostly by young women, none of whom looked as old to Rhodes as his own daughter. And they were often chatting back and forth and always telling their customers to have a nice day. Things were a lot more cheerful in banks these days. All the tellers had computers at their stations, too. No more adding machines.

Some things hadn't changed, however. The bank president still had the nicest office, the deepest carpet, the biggest desk, and the most windows. He still wore a dark suit and behaved with reserve and restraint.

"And why do you need this information, Sheriff?" he said.

"It's part of a murder investigation, Mr. Freer," Rhodes explained.

Freer was president of the Clearview Interbank, sixty years old, compact and athletic, with a tanned face that Rhodes was sure came from a lamp rather than the sun. He had survived the takeover of the Clearview State Bank by one of the big holding companies, one of the few bank officers to do so. He had not achieved his present position by being free with information.

"I'd rather do this informally," Rhodes went on. "Easier on both of us." They both knew that bank records were no big secret these days and that Rhodes could get access to them without having to go to much trouble.

"All right," Freer said. "I don't really need to look at the records. I can tell you that Sunny Dale is having a bit of difficulty now."

"What kind of difficulty?" Rhodes asked.

"It's a little unusual in that it's a privately operated institution," Freer said. "Many nursing homes now are operated by large organizations which hire the managers and other employees for the individual homes."

"Like banks," Rhodes said.

Freer didn't think the remark was amusing. He didn't think a lot of things were amusing. "At any rate, Mr. Patterson is the owner of the institution. He inherited some money, I believe, and that allowed him to get started in the business. He had been a nurse, before."

Rhodes hadn't known that, but it seemed logical. Mr. Patterson somehow *looked* like a nurse. He had that competent, no-nonsense air.

"About that difficulty," he said, thinking of Dunstable. Getting information these days was like pulling teeth.

"He's had some trouble getting his money from one of the government programs—I don't know whether it's Medicare or Medicaid. He's behind on his note with the bank."

"How far behind?"

"Four months."

"Is that bad?"

"It isn't good. Not that there is any danger of foreclosure."

He didn't have to say why. Things had not been good in Texas for bankers lately, and Rhodes was sure that one thing the bank didn't need was a nursing home. Besides, four months probably wasn't really that far behind for someone who was sure to pay. Or was Patterson that sure to pay? Rhodes asked Freer about it.

"Oh, there's no doubt of it. He'll be getting the money. The government makes errors, or things get tangled in all the red tape, but the money will come through." He sounded completely confident.

Rhodes, when he left, wasn't so sure. What if Patterson was worried about the money? What if, for one thing, he

9 5

had committed some sort of Medicare fraud? Rhodes had read about places collecting on patients who had been dead for months, collecting on patients who had moved to other establishments. What if Patterson had been guilty of something like that? Would he try to get money by killing one of his own patients?

It was hard to believe. Patterson didn't seem the type to Rhodes, who tended to trust his judgments about people. But he had been fooled before. For every Ruth Grady, about whom he had been right, there was a Johnny Sherman, about whom he had been wrong.

Anyway, it was one more thing to check into.

It was nearly noon when Rhodes left the bank, so he went by his house for lunch. He and Ivy had eaten all the pimiento cheese last night, but there was bound to be something in the refrigerator, he thought.

There was nothing to eat, however, except for two slices of bologna that had fuzzy green-and-black mold growing in patches on them. Rhodes was not especially particular about what he ate, but he wasn't going to eat that. He threw the bologna away and made a peanut butter sandwich on the oat bran bread.

It wasn't bad.

As he ate, he thought about Hack and the reporter. There was still time to catch the noon news, so he switched on the little portable radio that he kept in the kitchen. It had terrible sound quality, but it was good enough to listen to the news on.

He had missed Red Rogers's introduction to the interview, in which the lawsuit was undoubtedly mentioned, but he got in on the first question.

"So, Mr. Jensen," Rogers said. "As the dispatcher at the Blacklin County Jail, what can you tell us about the conditions here?"

Hack's voice came through loud and clear. "Well, it's better eatin' than you can get anywhere except your mama's kitchen."

"Are you saying that you eat the same food that the prisoners get?"

"No, sir. I wish I did. They eat a lot better than I do."

Rogers decided to get off that topic. "What about the roof?"

"We got one, all right," Hack said.

"Is it a good one?"

"I expect so," Hack said. "I never looked at it, but it passed the last inspection."

"But does it leak?"

"Leak what?"

"Water," Rogers said. "When it rains."

"Not in here," Hack said.

"Ah, yes, but this is where the administrators stay. What about over the cells?"

Rhodes smiled through a bite of the peanut butter as he thought about the "administrators." He wondered if Hack had ever thought of himself as an administrator of the jail.

"You'd have to ask Lawton about the cells," Hack said. "He's the jailer."

Good, Rhodes thought. Lawton had come in. Served Red Rogers right for trying to stir up trouble.

"What about that, Mr. Lawton?" Rogers said.

"What about what?" Lawton said.

"The roof. Does it leak over the cells?"

"Sometimes," Lawton said.

"When would those times be?" Rogers said, pressing his luck.

"When the repairs wear out."

"Repairs? What repairs would those be?"

"The ones we do ever' time we find a leak. You think we want the prisoners to get wet?" Lawton asked.

"Let's talk about neglect," Rogers said, changing the

subject again. "Personal neglect of prisoners. Does any of that go on around here?"

"What's *neglect* mean?" Hack asked. "They eat good. They get a bed to sleep in. We don't make 'em work for their supper. We fix the roof when it leaks. That sound like neglect to you?"

"We don't tuck 'em in at night, though," Lawton said. "You got to admit that, Hack."

Rhodes looked for something to wash down the sandwich with. Rogers must have not had much time to do his editing. That was fine with Rhodes. He was enjoying the interview.

"Do they get to exercise?" Rogers said. "Prisoners have a right to exercise."

"We let 'em do all the exercise they want to," Lawton said. "Push-ups, sit-ups, leg lifts, they can do all of that. I never stopped a one of them."

"But were they supervised?" Rogers said.

"If they asked me to, I'd've supervised 'em."

"But did they ask you to?"

"Nope. But that ain't my fault, is it?"

Rhodes found about half of a two-liter bottle of Dr Pepper in the refrigerator. He opened it and poured some in a glass. It was flat, but he drank it anyway.

"What about a law library? Aren't prisoners supposed to have access to a law library?" Rhodes remembered that was also a part of Little Barnes's complaint.

"They got as much access as I have," Hack said. "How much do you think law books cost? You think the taxpayers want to provide law books for people we got in here for drunk drivin'? For people we got in here for stealin'? You radio newsmen sure have funny ideas about how people want to spend their tax money."

"There you have it, folks," Red Rogers said. Rhodes thought he detected a note of quiet desperation in the man's voice, but he wasn't sure. "Blacklin County has no

98

law library, no supervised exercise program, and a jail roof that leaks. If you have an opinion on this matter, you can call me here at the station and talk to all of Clearview on the air."

By the time Rhodes left home, the calls were running about five to one in favor not only of keeping things at the jail as they were, but for making them worse. Blacklin County wasn't a place where people liked the idea of coddling criminals.

Sneaking out of the jail was the smartest thing Rhodes had done all day. He was willing to bet that he wouldn't be bothered by Red Rogers again.

TEN

Rhodes had been thinking about the well where Louis Horn's body was supposedly dumped. Horn's car had been found down by the river, not far from the highway bridge, not that there had been much of a highway in those days. More like a rutted mud road, probably considerably churned up by the rain the night Horn had disappeared. But the bridge was still in more or less the same place, though it was no longer made of wood as it had been in Horn's time.

Not far from the bridge was the Old Settlers' Grounds, or what was left of it.

Even when Rhodes was a boy, the Old Settlers' Grounds was mostly just a memory. About the only thing left of the original grounds by then was a dance pavilion to which electricity had been run and where the Girl Scouts held square dances with whatever willing, or unwilling but nevertheless available, boys they could round up. A time or two, Rhodes recalled, he had been one of those boys.

He had been swimming there at the Grounds, too, in what remained of the two big swimming pools that had been constructed down by the river. There were times when the river water would flow in and boys would go down there and swing out over the pools on a long rope tied high in the branches of a giant pecan tree and let go and drop down into the cool green water.

No one went down there anymore. Too dangerous, Rhodes had heard. The old pool's concrete sides had crumbled, and anyone diving in was likely to hit his head on a chunk of it and drown. Dropping from a rope high above would have been unthinkable. And of course the river water was now a murky grayish-brown instead of a clear green, and God knows what chemicals it might contain. The whole place was overgrown with brush and trees, and there were no doubt snakes in plenty when the weather was warm.

There had been a time when there were swings and see-saws and men selling red hokey-pokey to drink. Kids yelling and having fun, parents worrying about them and watching.

Rhodes had missed all of that, though he had heard about it. All he remembered was the pavilion and the pool. And one other thing. The Wishing Well.

It had originally been a well for drinking water, so that thirsty picnickers and swimmers could refresh themselves, but by the time Rhodes saw it, it had long since been dry, not that anyone would have drunk out of it even if there had been water.

So it had become the Wishing Well, a place for the Girl Scouts and the boys from the square dances to visit and toss pennies in, wishing for whatever it was that kids in those days would have wished for. Rhodes knew that he had thrown more than one penny down that well, but for the life of him he couldn't remember his wishes.

The road to the Old Settlers' Grounds was still pretty much as it had been in the days when Rhodes was making those wishes, whatever they were. Just before the bridge, Rhodes turned off into two ruts with dead grass and some live weeds between them, the trees close on either side. There hadn't been much rain lately, so the ruts were packed hard. The bare tree limbs scratched along the side of the car as Rhodes drove.

It was less than a quarter of a mile from the highway to the gateway to the Grounds. There was an entrance arch of wrought-iron between two high wooden posts, one of which leaned precariously forward, throwing the arch askew. Rhodes could still read the words OLD SETTLERS' GROUNDS on the arch, however. He drove the car under the arch and onto the Grounds themselves.

He was not surprised to see that the grass around the old pavilion was mashed flat. He'd heard from the deputies that the Grounds were now used as a lover's lane by a lot of the Clearview high school kids. The deputies would roust them when there was nothing else to do, but even from the car Rhodes could see by the number of condom containers scattered around that some of the visitors to the Grounds had not been rousted before they had the opportunity to practice safe sex.

He stopped the car, got out, and walked down to the pavilion. The clearing was thickly overgrown with trees, and that plus the overcast sky made it almost dark. It was cold in the shadows, and looking at the old pavilion made Rhodes feel even colder.

The last time he had seen it, which must have been thirty years ago, it had not seemed in bad shape. It had been old, even then, but it had been solid. He could remember the sound of the feet shuffling on the floor as he and some girl did a do-si-do, the hard benches around the sides, the bare light bulb hanging from the roof and drawing hundreds of moths.

Now half of the roof was caved in, hanging dangerously low over a floor that was rotten and full of holes. The sides of the pavilion had fallen both inward and outward, and rotted wood lay on the grass and the floor. Rhodes had thought he might step up on the dance floor for old times' sake, but the steps were already broken and clearly would not hold his weight. He tried to remember the girls he had danced with there and wondered what they looked like now.

He shook off the feeling of nostalgia and thought about the Wishing Well. It had been down a slope, between the pavilion and the swimming pools. He walked around the dance floor. There appeared to be a path still running in that direction, though it was not as well defined as the ruts in the road. He started down the path, pushing the tree limbs out of his way with his hand.

The Wishing Well was there in a small clearing, all right, just about where he had remembered it. The grass around it was flattened out like the grass around the pavilion, but not by cars. Probably some of the lovers had taken blankets along and walked down the path looking for even more privacy than the clearing provided them.

Although the well was there, it did not look anything like Rhodes remembered it. He recalled crumbling brick sides covered with a thin layer of cement that had mostly fallen away, but the sides had still been several feet tall.

They were hardly that tall now. They were barely there at all, two or three bricks at most still showing above the ground. No evidence of the cement veneer remained.

However, there was something new. *Well*, Rhodes thought, *new probably isn't exactly the right word.*

There was a pecan tree growing right up out of the well, its branches spreading out over Rhodes's head. There were even quite a few pecans lying around on the ground. The people who visited the spot these days evidently were interested in things other than eating them.

Rhodes picked up two of the pecans and cracked them together in his right hand. He peeled back the cracked shell, pulled out the sweet meat, and popped it into his mouth, chewing it as he looked at the tree.

Even more than the decayed pavilion, the tree gave him

the impression of the passing years. At some time in the past, maybe even while he had been coming there, an industrious squirrel had dropped a nut into the well. Or maybe some kid Rhodes's own age had thrown it in, not having a penny to spend on wishes. Against all the odds, it had gotten covered over with enough dirt to sprout and take root, maybe as a result of a rain storm, maybe as the result of animal activity.

Rhodes wondered if a squirrel had fallen in the well and been unable to get out. It was possible.

At any rate, there was the tree, and not a scrawny one, growing high out of the well, a tree that had grown that tall, that strong, in the years since Rhodes had been there. It gave him a funny feeling, since it didn't really seem that long ago that he had thrown his own pennies in. There were days when it didn't seem more than a few months since he had been a teenager.

This wasn't one of those days. The tree made it seem more like a million years. The wind blew the tree branches, causing them to scrape together. Rhodes hunched his shoulders against the cold.

He wondered if this could possibly be the well that Mr. Bobbit had been talking about. It made sense. It was certainly close enough to where Horn's car had been found. It wouldn't have been hard for a man of Kennedy's size to carry a body down here, especially if he had a little help. Lloyd Bobbit had been small, but he had probably been tough and strong in his younger days.

The well was not deep. Having been so close to the river, it had probably not needed to be. Rhodes had looked into it more than once when throwing his money in, looked to see the other pennies that were lying on the bottom. It would be possible to dig down beside it and see what was there. There had probably been enough water in it in Louis Horn's time to cover a body.

Rhodes thought for a second about that, about the tree

being fertilized by the remains of the son of Dry Hole Horn. Then he dismissed the thought. By the time the tree had started to grow, there hadn't been enough left of Horn to do much fertilizing.

There was no statute of limitations on murder, and that was another problem. If he did discover a body, it was not going to be easy to prosecute anyone, not even Kennedy. If they could find him.

And finding remains wouldn't mean they had found Horn. There would be difficulty in identifying whatever they found.

Rhodes looked through the trees at the river. It flowed sluggishly along, its waters muddier than he remembered having seen them lately. The lines of concrete that marked the old swimming pools were barely visible. The pools themselves were mostly filled in with dirt and leaves, another change that Rhodes hadn't been prepared for. He'd thought that there might still be a little river water in them. He supposed it wasn't so surprising that they had filled with silt, however, not after the tree. It had been a long time since he'd been there, sure enough.

Then Rhodes heard something moving in the trees behind him.

At first he thought it was just the wind, but then he heard it again. Someone was walking across the dry, dead leaves, trying hard not to be heard but making a little noise nevertheless.

It could have been a couple of lovers looking for a private spot to spread a blanket, but Rhodes didn't think so. This was hardly the kind of day anyone would choose for outdoor lovemaking.

He stood still, listening, but the noises had stopped.

That didn't mean that whoever was making them had stopped moving, however. He might have just gotten quieter.

Rhodes looked all around him, trying to get a glimpse of

something that was out of place among the trees. It wasn't easy. Although the trees were mostly bare except for some of the oaks, they were thick, and there were many bushes growing among them. The bushes were evergreens of some kind, and they grew as thick as the trees. It would be easy for someone to hide, using them for cover, especially in the near-dark conditions.

There was no reason for Rhodes to suspect that anyone coming to the Old Settlers' Grounds would intend him harm, but the flesh was crawling between his shoulder blades.

It wasn't the cold, either. He suddenly realized that someone had been watching him for some minutes, maybe ever since he had walked down to the Wishing Well.

He thought about the Grounds, wondering just for a minute if he might be trespassing. But then he remembered that the Blacklin county owned this property. Every now and then, someone would propose to the county commissioners that the Grounds be restored. And of course, the state owned the river banks, up to a certain distance from the center of the river. At any rate, as a taxpayer and county resident, Rhodes had as much right to be there as anyone. Maybe more, since he was the sheriff.

"Who's there?" he called. He didn't really expect anyone to answer, but he thought he might stir up some action.

His words were lost on the wind. The only reply he got was the sound of the tree branches scratching one another and the stirring of oak leaves.

He moved cautiously in the direction he thought the sound had come from. He did not like to draw his pistol, but he did. There was no need to take unnecessary chances.

Just as he got into the trees, he caught sight of a flash of red moving away from him, down toward the river. It looked like a red coat or shirt of some kind, and Rhodes headed in that direction.

He was not an expert woodsman, and his feet kept getting tangled in vines. Thorns seemed to reach for him, and he walked headlong into spider webs that covered his face and stuck to his skin. Once he almost fell and had to grab hold of a limb to keep himself upright. He holstered the pistol then. Dropping it would be a big mistake.

He probably wasn't making any more noise than the average elephant stampede. If there really had been anyone in front of him, whoever it was sure wouldn't have any trouble hearing him coming.

He came out of the trees near the swimming pools. The bank of the river was fairly clear of trees here. There were two or three towering oaks, and Rhodes was sure that one of them was where the rope he had dropped from had once been tied, though there was no sign of it now.

There was no sign of anyone wearing a red coat, either. There was no sign of anyone at all. A squirrel chattered away in the top of one of the oaks, but besides that and the north wind there was no other sound.

Rhodes walked to where he could see into one of the pools. No one was hiding in it, though he hadn't really thought anyone would be. There wasn't any place to hide. The dead leaves and dirt were piled too high, even in the pool's deepest end.

Rhodes looked out across the river. There had once been a bridge here, a narrow wooden affair that had allowed people to cross over to the other side of the river and sit at picnic tables under the trees there.

There was no bridge there now, no way for anyone to cross. It would have been easy enough for someone to circle back around behind Rhodes and get back to the well or pavilion without being seen, however. Rhodes looked back up in the direction of the Wishing Well, but he did not see anyone among the trees.

He looked back at the pool. He wondered how long it

had been since boys had been swimming there. It took a lot of years for a pool that deep to fill up with dirt and trash. No wonder there had been no sign of the rope he had once swung from. It had no doubt rotted away long ago.

For just a moment the chill of the air went away, and Rhodes seemed to hear in his mind the sound of boys laughing and splashing in the waters of the pool. He could almost see the warm drops of water flash in the sun as one of the boys swung out over the pool, let go of a rope, and made the long drop into the pool. He could feel the rough rope in his hands, feel the warm air rushing past him as he fell.

He almost didn't hear the sound behind him until it was too late.

As it was, he managed to half turn and catch most of the blow of the heavy tree limb on his shoulder rather than on the back of his head as had been intended.

Pain shot down his left arm, and his whole upper body went numb. He felt himself falling, but there was nothing he could do to stop.

He heard about the dangers of nostalgia, but this was ridiculous, he thought as he fell.

He landed hard and rolled over, just in time to avoid another blow from the tree-limb club. It smashed into the ground beside his head with a heavy thud.

Rhodes looked up to see who was trying to bash his head in, but all he could see was the club coming at him again.

He rolled to the left. His shoulder felt as if someone were sticking a knife in it, but he ignored the pain and tried to get to his feet. It wasn't easy. He found it hard to get his balance with his arm hanging limp.

He didn't make it up. He wasn't fast enough. The club hit him again, this time across his shoulders. He pitched forward, scraping his face in the dirt. His back felt broken.

That wasn't the worst of his problems. Whoever was

clubbing him was going to kill him if he didn't do something fast.

And he couldn't move fast at all, not now.

He did manage to roll over on his back and look up.

What he saw was an old man in a red hunting jacket, an old man with slightly protruding teeth and a club, a club that he was swinging at Rhodes's head again.

Rhodes was never going to say anything about old men who couldn't move fast. This one was moving all *too* fast for Rhodes's peace of mind.

Rhodes rolled over twice and drew his pistol. He hardly got it out before the tree branch slammed it out of his hand. It sailed off into the pool. Rhodes didn't hear it land. He was too busy worrying about the fingers of his right hand, which felt as if they had been wrenched out of joint or maybe broken by the club.

The old man swinging the branch did seem to be tiring, however. He let the club drop to his side while he tried to get his breath. Rhodes could hear him wheezing. That seemed to be Rhodes's only hope, to let the old man beat on him until he tired himself out.

Rhodes tried again to get to his feet. He didn't feel much better than the old man. In fact, he probably felt a lot worse. He hadn't laid a finger on the man, whereas he had been hit three times. So far.

As soon as he staggered to his feet, he realized that getting up had not been as good an idea as it had seemed. The old man—it had to be Maurice Kennedy—had been at least halfway bluffing. He was not nearly as tired as he had seemed. He had just wanted a better shot at Rhodes. He wasn't doing too well swinging down at the ground.

He did better now, at least from his point of view. He swung the club at Rhodes's chest like a major leaguer clean-up hitter swinging a bat at a fat change-up.

Rhodes tried to raise his hands, but it was no good. The tree branch connected with his chest and all the air went

110

out of him. He staggered backward, trying to get his breath, felt his heels click against the concrete edge of the pool, and then felt himself falling, his good arm waving uselessly in the air.

Then something hit him in the back of the head and he didn't feel anything at all.

CHAPTER
ELEVEN

Rhodes was sailing across a vast open space, clinging to a rope, his hands gripping it hard just above a large knot. A frayed end dangled underneath the knot, and far below Rhodes was the water of the pool shimmering greenly in the sunlight.

But it was too far below. Much too far. Instead of ten or twelve feet, as it should have been, it seemed like miles, and the longer he clung to the rope, the more the pool receded in the distance below him. When he had first looked, it had been the size of a real pool, stretching out twenty feet on either side. But now it looked more the size of a school book, and as he watched, it shrank to the size of a postage stamp.

He couldn't tell whether the pool was moving down or the rope was being pulled upward. There was no real sensation of motion.

He could hear voices, voices that he did not recognize, yelling at him, telling him to let go of the rope, but the more they yelled, the tighter his grip became. After a few minutes, he tried to climb the rope, but his hands were sweaty and he kept slipping back down to the knot.

Suddenly, without warning, the rope broke and he was plunging downward, moving faster and faster. The pool had receded so far from him that now it was not even visible.

He threw out his arms and jerked his body upward, trying to reach the tree branch high above him, though he knew that it was hopeless, and that was when he woke up.

He was lying on his back in the pool, stretched out on a bed of leafcovered dirt. It was a lot softer than you would expect it to be, but Rhodes hurt all over. He felt as if he'd fought a few rounds with Hit Man Hearns, who had gotten tired and turned him over to a grizzly bear.

His left arm hurt, his back hurt, his chest hurt, and most of all his head hurt. It felt as if there were someone in there pounding away with a rubber mallet on the inside of his skull, especially at the back. There was another little man inside his left shoulder, which was throbbing almost as much as his head.

He tried to sit up, and his head swelled with pain, seeming to balloon to twice its normal size. He reached back and felt a tender spot, brushing it lightly with his fingers. Even that hurt, and his fingers came away damp with blood.

He looked behind him. There didn't seem to be anything hard there, but when he brushed away the leaves there was a chunk of concrete from the pool's side just beneath them.

He got to his feet with considerable effort and then looked around for his pistol. He didn't find it.

The wall of the pool was only about two feet above where he stood, but for a minute he wondered if he could step up there and get out. Then he did it, but he had to stand for a while and get his breath back. He didn't even consider trying to brush the dirt off his jacket and pants or to remove the dead leaves that still clung to him.

He looked around him carefully. His pistol wasn't there, either.

After a time that might have been ten minutes or thirty, he started walking up to the Wishing Well. When he got there, he stopped to rest again. He was feeling a little better, however, and he was also feeling stupid. How could he have let someone sneak up on him like that?

Getting caught up in old memories was counterproductive in more ways than one. Now Maurice Kennedy had a pistol.

As Rhodes discovered when he got back to the pavilion, Kennedy had a car, too. The county car was no longer parked where it had been, and when Rhodes reached in his pocket he discovered that the keys were gone.

He sat down on one of the less rotted portions of the pavilion steps and thought about things. The cold air seemed to be helping his head, and the throbbing in his arm had almost stopped.

He didn't know where Kennedy had been staying since leaving Sunny Dale, but he probably hadn't spent too much time at the Old Settlers' Grounds. It was too cold, for one thing, and there was no place to get out of the night air. It was just bad luck that he had happened to be there when Rhodes was looking at the well.

The fact that he *was* there, though, would seem to lend credence to the elder West's story about the dumping of Louis Horn's body. If there were indeed traces of the body still buried in that well, then Kennedy certainly had a strong motive for killing Lloyd Bobbit, assuming that what West had overheard was true. Since Bobbit had been with Kennedy on the night of the murder, everything seemed to fit.

Now all Rhodes had to do was find Kennedy, who was on the loose with a pistol and a county car. It was really too bad about the car. It was the same one that Rhodes had recently wrecked. The commissioners hadn't liked that much, even if the wreck hadn't really been Rhodes's fault, and they certainly weren't going to like having it stolen.

Things like that tended to increase the county's insurance rates. Of course, they had a lot of other things on their minds, like the lawsuit, and might not have time to worry about a minor matter like a stolen car.

Rhodes got up. Before he could do anything about Kennedy, or anything else, he had to get back to town. At least his legs weren't hurting. They were about the only thing that wasn't.

He took a deep breath and started walking.

He didn't have to go far, which was a good thing. He didn't think he could have made it much farther than the highway, which is where he caught a ride with a man on his way to town in a pickup truck. The man was going in to the hospital emergency room to have a boil lanced, and he was a lot more interested in discussing his own troubles than inquiring into Rhodes's, which was all right with the sheriff.

The man let Rhodes off at the jail, where Hack and Lawton were still talking about their appearance on the noon news when he walked in the door. They stopped as soon as they got a good look at him, however.

"My God," Hack said. "You look like you got run over by a Mack truck."

"Or a locomotive." Lawton said.

Rhodes eased himself into his chair. He told them what had happened. He didn't even feel like drawing out the story to give them a dose of their own medicine.

"I guess Ruth won't be havin' too much to say about old men, now," Hack said. Rhodes thought he detected a note of pride in the dispatcher's voice. "'Course you ain't so young yourself anymore."

"That's what got me into this mess," Rhodes told him. "Thinking about when I was younger." He reached up to touch the back of his head.

"I expect you got a concussion," Hack said.

"Maybe broken ribs, too," Lawton said. "What you need to do is see a doctor."

"I will," Rhodes told them, "but not until we get out a bulletin on the car." He leaned back in his chair while Hack put out the bulletin on the radio. Before Hack was through, Rhodes was asleep.

He woke up in the hospital. It was dark in the room, but he knew by the smell where he was. He sat up and fumbled around for a light switch.

"I'm glad you're finally awake," Ivy Daniel said. There was a click, and the room light came on. "I was getting worried."

"What time is it?" Rhodes said.

"Nearly ten o'clock. You've slept for quite a while."

"How did I get here?"

"Ruth Grady brought you, with a little help from Hack and Lawton."

Rhodes didn't feel much better, in spite of the sleep he'd gotten. He was still sore all over. He sat up and felt the back of his head, where there seemed to be an odd lump. He touched smooth skin and a fresh bandage.

"You have a mild concussion," Ivy said. "They shaved the back of your head and took a few stitches. Four, I think. Maybe five. Not many."

"What about my—"

"Your chest is badly bruised, but no ribs were broken. Your back seems fine, except that you're bruised there, too."

Rhodes looked at her. Her mouth was tight with disapproval.

"I need to get to the jail," he said.

"You're not going anywhere, not for a day or two. The

117

doctor said that if you didn't have such a hard head you might be dead."

Rhodes wondered whether she was worried about him or mad at him. He couldn't quite tell, so he asked her.

"I don't know," she said. "I haven't decided yet."

He knew what she meant, or thought he did. She knew that he was a lawman, but she hadn't yet accepted the fact that his job was sometimes, though not very often, dangerous. It was something that she was going to have to get used to.

"I don't want to get used to it," she said, as if reading his mind. "I don't want to think that I might find myself standing in front of the county judge next Friday, waiting for a man who might not show up because he's getting himself beaten up by some old man with a tree limb."

"Hack tells too much," Rhodes said. "And speaking of Hack, I have to find out about the county car. And I need to talk to Ruth Grady."

"Don't you try to change the subject," Ivy said.

Rhodes hadn't really been trying to change the subject, not consciously. "I have to do my job," he said.

"Not when you're in the hospital."

Rhodes lay back against the pillows. "You can't keep me here until Friday."

"I know. I'd like to, though." Ivy smiled faintly, and Rhodes felt a little better.

He looked over at the night stand by the bed. There was an afternoon Clearview paper lying there, and he could see part of the headline. He reached for the paper and unfolded it.

FORMER INMATE SUES COUNTY, SHERIFF, the headline read.

"Great," Rhodes said. "I wonder what Hack and Lawton think about this."

"They're disappointed because their names weren't in the headline," Ivy said. "That's what they told me, anyway."

118

"I imagine the commissioners are disappointed too, but not about that," Rhodes said.

He read the story. It wasn't nearly as bad as he had expected, and it did mention one thing he didn't know, that the commissioners were planning to call in a team of structural engineers to see if the jail was sound. "If it is," Commissioner James Allen was quoted as saying, "then there will be no need to call for a bond election. We can repair the present facility, and with a few minor changes it will continue to serve us well."

That must have been something the commissioners had decided on after Rhodes had talked to Allen. It made sense. If the jail was structurally sound, and if the engineers certified that it was, then they could fix the roof, maybe even air condition the cells. Get an exercise yard built behind the jail. Buy a computer system. Maybe he wouldn't have to worry about a new jail after all.

There was a photograph of the jail accompanying the article. The old building didn't look half bad. In fact, it looked good for another eighty or so years.

Rhodes looked for the story on Lloyd Bobbit's murder. He knew it would be there. Ordinarily, a murder was big news in Blacklin County and would certainly have rated a headline above the fold. This time, however, the article had been crowded down to the bottom of the page, for which Rhodes was thankful. Most people probably wouldn't even notice it.

He put the paper down. "I still have to talk to Ruth," he said, reaching for the telephone.

Ruth Grady was off duty, but Rhodes reached her at home. She had done everything he had asked her to do, and more.

She had found the county car, too.

"It was in the Wal-Mart parking lot," she said. "The keys

119

were in it. Whoever took it just left it there and walked away."

That seemed to mean that Kennedy was still in the county.

"What about my pistol?" Rhodes said.

"That wasn't there," Ruth told him. "Sorry."

Rhodes sighed. He hadn't really expected it to be. That would have been asking too much. At least they had the car back, unharmed.

"Was the shotgun still in the car?"

"Yes. Lucky for us it's not so easy to get to."

It might not be easy to get to in an emergency, either, but that didn't matter to Rhodes right now. He was just glad it was still in the car.

"Did you get a chance to talk to Foley and Everett?" he said.

She had talked to both of them. Dave Foley was a truck driver for a grocery company. His mother was in Sunny Dale, and he had visited her around the time Lloyd Bobbit had died. However, he said that he didn't know Bobbit, didn't even know who he was. His mother's room was on the other hall, and he had never even been near Bobbit's room. As far as Ruth could determine, he was telling the truth.

Lyle Everett was another story. His mother was in Sunny Dale, too, but there was a definite connection between her and Bobbit. She had dated him when they were both much younger. Her maiden name was Lansing.

Rhodes thought he recalled seeing that name in the old records relating to the disappearance of Louis Horn.

"You probably did," Ruth said. "I talked to her. She was there that night."

Rhodes couldn't think of any reason why Everett might kill Bobbit, however, unless it was the fact that Bobbit had threatened his mother the way he had threatened Kennedy.

"She says he didn't threaten her. According to her, they hadn't talked for weeks, maybe longer," Ruth said.

"That's about what I'd say, too, if murder was involved and I was being questioned," Rhodes said. He knew they would have to check it out, no matter how likely a suspect Kennedy was. "What about the dentists?"

According to Ruth, the dentist who had made Bobbit's teeth was a Dr. Billy Richards. "He says that, sure, Kennedy could have used the teeth. But it wouldn't be very sanitary, and they wouldn't fit well at all. They'd probably be very uncomfortable, maybe even painful."

Rhodes thought about the man who had attacked him, about the way his teeth had protruded slightly from his lips.

"Why would he want them, then?" he said.

"Maybe because he'd lost his own and didn't want to be fitted for others. Richards checked his records, and he made a set of dentures for Kennedy about six years ago. He remembers Kennedy as just about the most contrary customer he's ever had."

Rhodes told Ruth what a good job she'd done and hung up the phone. He had a lot to think about, or rather, to talk about, since Ivy was still there. She sometimes had good ideas about his cases, and it always helped to talk to her about them.

He told her what he thought might have happened—that Kennedy had lost his own dentures and taken Bobbit's, that Bobbit had threatened to tell the story of Louis Horn's death if the teeth weren't returned, and that Kennedy had killed him to shut him up.

"Kennedy was probably out there at the Old Settlers' Grounds today checking to see if anyone had talked to Bobbit before he was killed, to see if we were investigating the Wishing Well. When he saw me, he decided to get rid of me right there."

"He nearly did, too," Ivy said, shaking her head.

"Well, like the doctor said, I've got a thick skull. I've got to get out of here and find Kennedy."

"From what Hack says, you didn't have much luck at that even before you were concussed. It won't hurt you to spend the night here, at the very least. You can play Sergeant Preston again tomorrow."

That was one of the many reasons Rhodes liked Ivy. She remembered things like Sergeant Preston.

"And just what are you planning to do when you get out, anyway?" she asked. "You're not in any condition to go running around the countryside looking for anyone, not even an old man."

"I'm not going to run. I think the next stop is to dig down by that well and see if we can find anything. If we do, then we go after Kennedy even harder."

"What if you don't?"

"That doesn't mean Kennedy didn't kill Bobbit, or Horn either. We still have to find him."

"He's the number one suspect," Ivy said.

"That's exactly right."

"But not the only one."

"No," Rhodes said. "Not the only one. There's still the daughter, but I think we can rule her out. She had power of attorney, and now that Bobbit's dead, that's ended. The money will be tied up until the will goes through probate. If anything, she's worse off. We still have to check out Lyle Everett, though. It's just possible that he's involved some-how." He went on to explain that Everett's mother had been at the dance where Louis Horn was killed. "Her maiden name was Lansing."

"Faye Lansing," Ivy said. "That name was in the records of the investigation, all right."

Rhodes was glad to have his own memory confirmed.

"It seems like a pretty tenuous connection, though," Ivy said.

Rhodes agreed that it was. "But you never know," he said. "You just never know."

They talked a little longer, about the wedding and other things, but Rhodes could tell that Ivy was still upset with him for getting himself beat up. First the lawsuit, now this. Things weren't going well on the romance front.

When she left to go home, she didn't kiss him good night.

She did promise him that she would feed Speedo, however. It was nice to know that she still liked his dog.

CHAPTER
TWELVE

The next morning, Rhodes was still sore. He managed to get out of bed and dress himself, but every time he bent his left arm he could almost feel the tree branch slamming into him. The doctor tried to talk him into staying another day, but he didn't listen. He just promised to be careful and not to get hit again.

Ruth Grady picked him up at the hospital and drove him out to the Old Settlers' Grounds. It was still cold, but the overcast had blown away and the sun was shining through the trees as they drove down to the pavilion. There was a truck parked there; it had towed a long, low flatbed trailer, but there was nothing on the trailer now.

"I guess James is down at the well already," Rhodes said as they got out of the car. He felt about a hundred years old because it was so painful to move. Stretching his shoulders caused all the muscles in his chest and back to hurt. The wind felt funny, blowing on the back of his head where the bandage was.

They could hear the backhoe machine chugging as they walked down toward the well. Rhodes had called Allen from the hospital and asked him for a favor; Allen was glad to oblige.

"Be a good way to get out of going to church," he said. It seemed that there was a feud among the congregation, about half of them wanting to get rid of the preacher and the other half wanting to keep him. Because Allen was in politics, people seemed to expect him to take sides and lead the charge one way or the other.

"I've got enough political troubles on the job," Allen said. "I don't like having to deal with them at the church. Rather drive a backhoe."

They saw the ugly yellow backhoe with Allen at the controls. He was wearing his work clothes, faded jeans, a green-and-black plaid mackinaw, and leather work gloves. There was already a large mound of damp, dark-brown dirt piled beside the machine.

As they watched, Allen came up with a scoop of dirt, swung the scoop around, and dumped the dirt on the pile. Clods tumbled down the side of the pile and rolled across the dead grass. The scoop moved back over the hole and dived in.

When they got down to the well, Allen waved to them and kept digging. Rhodes looked into the hole. It was already seven or eight feet deep. He didn't figure the well was much more than fifteen feet deep, if that.

"How much longer?" he said to Allen. He had to yell over the noise of the backhoe's engine.

Allen shrugged and yelled something that sounded like "About an hour or so."

There was nothing to do but wait. Rhodes and Ruth went back up to the pavilion where they could talk and sat down on the steps. Ruth explained that she had looked for Kennedy earlier that morning.

"I know he must be somewhere in town," she said. "Otherwise, why bring the car back there? But I can't figure out where he's staying. I checked the motels again.

He's not there, that's for sure. Not unless he's got some-body lying for him."

"He has to eat, too," Rhodes said.

"Darn," Ruth said. "I didn't think of that. I should've checked the restaurants. I wonder how much money he had?"

"Probably not much," Rhodes said. "Why don't you go back to town and see what you can turn up. Take a couple of hours, and then come on back here."

Ruth stood up and tugged on her gunbelt. The deputies always wore uniforms, though Rhodes never did. "Want me to stop by the jail and get you a pistol?" she said.

"That might not be a bad idea," Rhodes agreed. "Kennedy's got one."

She got in the car, backed it around, and drove off toward the highway. Rhodes got up slowly and walked back down to see if Allen was making any progress.

It was almost exactly two hours before they found Louis Horn. Or what was left of him. Or what was left of *somebody*.

Allen had begun digging toward the well when he came to the depth they estimated would be about the bottom. He came up with a few bricks in his first scoop, indicating that he had indeed broken through the side of the well, and then he ran into the tree roots.

The roots made the going a little tougher, but on the second scoop after that he brought up the leg bone.

It didn't look much like most people probably thought bones were supposed to look. It wasn't white and shiny; it was almost as brown as the dirt. But there was no mistaking what it was.

It was in the middle of the scoopful of dirt, but Rhodes saw it as the earth was being dumped on the third pile that Allen had started. He yelled at Allen, who leaned forward to hear. When he understood what Rhodes was saying, he used the scoop to dig off a layer of dirt at a time, the big metal teeth curiously delicate at the task, until the bone was uncovered. Then he cut the engine and climbed down to see what he'd unearthed.

Rhodes felt a little bit like Hamlet in the graveyard, in Shakespeare's play that he'd been forced to attend a performance of when he was in high school. His English teacher had driven the school bus to Dallas, and three classes of students had suffered through three or four hours of the bard's great work.

Or pretended to suffer. Rhodes would never have admitted it then, but he had secretly enjoyed the play. He even understood most of the lines, having been coerced, thanks to the threat of daily pop tests in English class, to read the play over the period of the past several weeks.

He couldn't say that he knew the man whose leg bone he held in his hand, not the way Hamlet had known the jester whose skull he observed, but it gave him a strange feeling just the same. Yesterday he had been here thinking of how things had been when he was a boy, and now he was being reminded of what he would become when he was dead.

This whole business, from dealing with the old folks at Sunny Dale to finding what he suspected to be the bones of the long-dead Louis Horn, was getting to be too much a reminder of his own mortality. He was beginning to wonder what a mid-life crisis was and whether it was time for him to have one, if he wasn't having it already.

Ruth Grady came back while they were looking at the bone. She was carrying a Smith & Wesson chief's special and a shovel. She handed the pistol to Rhodes and said, "It seems like this happens to you a lot."

Rhodes didn't say anything. He knew what she meant.

She pointed the shovel at the bone. "Anybody we know?"

Rhodes was tempted to tell her it was poor Yorick, but

128

he didn't want to show off his education. "Louis Horn, maybe," he said. "It won't be easy to find out. Did you check out the restaurants?"

"Sure did. Kennedy, or somebody who looked a lot like your description of him, ate a taco at the Whataburger this morning. I knew he was still in town; now if we could just find him . . ."

"That won't be much easier than finding out if this belongs to Louis Horn," Rhodes said, holding up the leg bone. There were plenty of places in Clearview or nearby that Kennedy could hide, deserted buildings, barns, collapsing farm houses. "We can tell the restaurant workers to be on the look-out for him, though. That's one thing."

"I've already talked to the kids at the Whataburger," Ruth said. "Now I guess it's time to see if we can find the rest of Mr. X. I'd better get busy." She took off her gunbelt and laid it carefully on the ground away from the dirt piles.

Allen helped her down in the hole. He was tired from working the backhoe, and Rhodes wasn't capable of doing any digging. This wasn't the time to be chivalrous, and Ruth wouldn't have appreciated it anyway. Besides, she was small and therefore the only one really suited to the close-quarters work in the hole.

After another hour or so Ruth had managed to dig out nearly a complete skeleton, skull and all. That was all they found—bones. No belt buckles, no buttons from a shirt, no pieces of leather from shoes.

"Whoever dumped him in there probably stripped him first," Ruth said. Her face was streaked with mud, and her uniform was filthy, but she didn't seem to mind. She seemed quite happy with her part in the operation. "Do you think we'll ever be able to identify him?"

Rhodes didn't really see how it would be possible. Whoever Horn's dentist had been, if he'd even had one,

129

would be long dead by now, and the records would most likely not have been preserved.

"It's still a pretty sensational deal," Allen said. He was happy, too. "It'll give the paper something to write about instead of the lawsuit. I think we ought to go back to town and give the reporters a call, let 'em bring a photographer out here and get a few shots of the backhoe and the well and our hardworking law enforcement folks."

"Not to mention our hardworking commissioner from precinct three," Rhodes said.

"Yeah," Allen said, smiling. "That, too."

Rhodes didn't have the energy to object. Allen had done him a favor, after all, and this would be his chance to pay it back.

"You can drive me back to the jail," he told Ruth. "I'll make the call, and you can come back out here for the picture taking."

"Don't take a bath or anything," Allen said. "And don't put on a clean uniform. We want this to look good."

"What about the bones?" Ruth said. "After the pictures, of course," she added, looking at Allen.

"Take them to Ballinger's," Rhodes said. "This is just like one of those books he reads. He'll like it even more than the newspaper will. And he'll know what to do with them."

"Nice kid," Allen observed as Ruth walked over to put on her belt. "She's dating one of the other commissioner's boys."

"I didn't know that," Rhodes said. It seldom occurred to him to think about the private lives of his deputies. It didn't surprise him that Ruth was dating, however. She was young and attractive. If he had thought about it at all, he would have been surprised if she hadn't been going out with someone.

"Sammy Hensley," Allen said. "Teaches history at the junior high."

Love in bloom, Rhodes thought. Hack, Ruth, even me. Old, young, middle-aged. Maybe life was the same no matter what age you were.

Unless you were Louis Horn. Or Lloyd Bobbit.

It took Rhodes a while to catch up on events from Saturday night, especially since one of the calls involved someone going swimming.

"That's pretty unusual for February," Rhodes admitted. He was sitting in his chair, leaning back with his eyes almost closed. The morning at the Wishing Well had tired him out more than he would have liked to admit. "But there's no law against swimming, is there?"

He didn't really feel like going through this. When he died, he would surely be rewarded for having suffered a great deal of his punishment on earth.

"Depends on where you're swimmin'," Hack said.

Rhodes waited. He wasn't going to try drawing him out.

"It wasn't the municipal pool," Lawton said. "They drain that in the winter."

"He knows that," Hack said. He didn't like it when Lawton tried to muscle in on the story. "Besides," he went on, "there was all that about the footsteps."

"Yeah," Lawton said. "That was what got it all started. The footsteps."

"What footsteps?" Rhodes said, hating himself. He blamed it on the pain in his shoulder.

"The ones on the roof," Lawton said.

"The apartment house roof," Hack added. He wasn't going to let Lawton take over.

The apartment house must have been the crucial point, since neither one of them would say anything after that. Hack sat at his desk and Lawton leaned against the wall, a broom handle in his hands. Occasionally he scraped the broom on the floor. They both looked at Rhodes expectantly. He watched them from under half-closed lids.

131

"All right," he said after a minute. They always won in the end. "What does the apartment house roof have to do with swimming in February?"

"Drunk guy," Hack said. "He was runnin' across the apartment house roof to jump in the swimmin' pool."

"Don't see how he could hit it, myself," Lawton said. "Had to jump off an eave, kinda at an angle, and even then he just barely missed the other edge of the roof where it squares off around the pool. It's just a little bitty pool. Looks like he'd've missed and hit the concrete."

Rhodes thought fleetingly about his dream.

"Didn't, though," Hack said. "The Lord takes care of idiots and drunks. That's what they say."

"Not near all of them," Lawton said. "How many highway fatalities did we have in the county last year? And ever' one of 'em caused by drunks."

"What about *this* drunk?" Rhodes said, trying to get them back on the subject.

"Oh, him," Hack said. "He's up in one of the cells. It wasn't easy gettin' him out of that scuba gear, though."

"Scuba gear?" Rhodes said. Vaudeville wasn't dead, he decided wearily. It had just moved off the stage and into the small-town jails.

"That's how they caught him," Hack said. "He got tired of jumpin' off the roof, finally. When the deputy got to the apartment house, the guy was layin' on the bottom of the pool, sound asleep. Breathin' with his scuba gear."

"I hope he doesn't get pneumonia in the cell," Rhodes said. "You two can't afford another million-dollar lawsuit. Neither can I."

"Don't worry," Lawton said. "I gave him an extra blanket."

There were any number of things Rhodes knew that he should be doing, including talking to Lyle Everett, but he didn't feel up to them. He wanted to have another conversation with Mr. West, too. There was something about their first talk that had bothered him, though he couldn't put his finger on exactly what it was. And he wanted to see the Stuarts. If there was anyone who could keep him up to date on the Sunny Dale gossip, it was them. Maybe they had heard something more about Kennedy and Bobbit.

Instead, he went home and watched fifteen minutes of *Sherlock Holmes and the Spider Woman* before he fell asleep on the couch.

The doorbell woke him. He was momentarily disoriented and looked around the darkening room to make sure he wasn't still in the hospital or at the jail. The TV screen anchored him, however. The second Sherlock Holmes feature of the afternoon was coming to an end. Rhodes thought it was *Sherlock Holmes Faces Death*, but he wasn't sure.

The doorbell rang again, and then someone started knocking on the facing. Rhodes heaved himself off the couch, stifling a groan, and walked to the front door, turning on a light on the way.

When he opened the door, Miss Bobbit was standing there. The light reflected off the lenses of her glasses as she shook her head at him.

"I hope you're not trying to avoid me, Sheriff," she said. "They told me at the jail that they didn't know where you were, but I knew better. I knew I could find you at home."

At least Hack and Lawton had tried. "I wasn't trying to avoid anyone, Miss Bobbit," Rhodes said. "Would you like to come in?" He stood aside and held the door open.

Miss Bobbit looked up at him suspiciously, but she stepped inside. "I want to know what you're doing about my father's death," she said. "I haven't heard a word since Friday night."

Rhodes walked over to his recliner. "Have a seat, Miss

Bobbit," he said, indicating the couch. He sat in the chair, not really caring whether she sat or not.

She did, however, and regarded him solemnly. "Well?" she said, putting her shoulder bag on the floor by her feet.

"Well," he said, "I found out those 'stories' about your father and Maurice Kennedy were true, for one thing."

She sat up straight. "How dare you! All of this started with my father's teeth! You're supposed to be looking for Kennedy, not digging up the past. I want that man arrested, and I want him arrested immediately."

She didn't know just how literally that past had been dug up.

"I was looking for a motive," Rhodes said. "I think I found one. Your father may have known about a murder Kennedy committed years ago. He may have been killed to silence him. It wasn't the teeth at all. Or if it was, that was only a little bit of it."

She didn't say anything. Rhodes thought that her chin might have quivered, but that was the only sign of emotion he could detect. He thought Miss Bobbit was a pretty cold fish.

"And another thing," he said. "You didn't mention that you and Andy West were going together."

"We're engaged," Miss Bobbit said. "I don't see that my fiancé has anything to do with my father's death."

"I didn't say he did," Rhodes said, wondering why West had not mentioned that little fact. "But his father happens to have the room right next door to where your father was killed. I just thought that was interesting." He decided not to tell her that West Senior had overheard the conversation between Kennedy and her father.

"That's how I met Andy," she said. "Because our fathers had adjoining rooms. We talked in the hallway one day, and we just seemed to hit it off."

Rhodes tried, but somehow he just couldn't imagine Brenda Bobbit "hitting it off" with anybody. It wasn't that

134

she was physically unattractive, though she was—at least she was to Rhodes. It was that she seemed cold, distant, and thoroughly self-centered. It seemed to Rhodes that even her father's death meant little to her. She was concerned with finding Kennedy, true, but only because of the affront the murder was to her personally. The fact that her father was dead seemed beside the point.

He remembered how she had acted when her father had disappeared, how she wanted him found at once and how she wanted everything kept out of the papers. She didn't want her name associated with unpleasant publicity. That was too bad, because as soon as the discovery of the bones at the Old Settlers' Grounds became public knowledge there was going to be a lot of publicity. Even a reporter like Red Rogers was going to make the connection between the bones and Maurice Kennedy, and the Bobbit name would be dragged into the story not long after that.

He thought of something else. "Did you ever talk to your father about the night Louis Horn disappeared?"

"No," she said. "I did not. He had nothing to do with that. I don't see why you keep coming back to it."

Because, Rhodes thought, *it just might be important*. It had suddenly occurred to him that Miss Bobbit wasn't off the hook, after all. It was more than simply her coldness. It was the fact that she was just the kind of woman who could kill to avoid publicity.

What if her father had told her about threatening Kennedy? What if she saw the chance of the Horn murder being made public and decided to do something about it? If she could pin the murder on Kennedy, because of the business about the teeth, she would be off the hook. And after the will was probated she would have the money again, though she lost control of it with her father's death.

He couldn't say any of that to her, however. Instead, he made a mental note to find out from the lab as soon as he could exactly where that plastic grocery bag had come from. Hadn't she said she was on her way to the grocery store the day he was killed? What if she had been there first?

And then he told her about finding the bones.

For the first time, she showed definite emotion. She picked up her shoulder bag and clenched her hands on it. It was as if she were trying to compress the leather. "But you don't know whose bones they are, do you?" she said. "Not for sure."

"No," Rhodes admitted. "I don't. But I can't prevent the news people from speculating."

"You'd better," she said, standing up to go. "You'd just better."

Rhodes stood up, too, but he didn't bother to walk her to the door. She slammed it so hard behind her that the glass rattled in the windows.

CHAPTER
THIRTEEN

After Miss Bobbit left, Rhodes went outside and fed Speedo. The dog was glad to see him and wanted to play, but Rhodes was too sore for running and roughhousing. There was a high, cold moon and a lot of icy stars, which Rhodes didn't feel like looking at for long.

He went back inside and called Ivy. She didn't want to come over. She was sure he needed his rest. He was beginning to wonder whether they were really going to get married on Friday or not, but he was too tired to worry about it. He went to bed early. He didn't even try to watch a movie. If he dreamed, he didn't remember it the next day.

The phone rang early. It was Hack, telling him that Ruth had been checking on Kennedy's whereabouts already that morning and that Mr. Patterson had called from Sunny Dale. "Wouldn't say what he wanted. Just said they'd found something you needed to see."

"I'll go on over there," Rhodes said. "Anything else?"

"Well, there was a shootin' incident last night, or a reported one. Nobody got shot, far's I know. The only interestin' thing is where it was."

"Where was it, then?"

"Out by Andy West's store. We got one of those anonymous calls that shots were bein' fired, but when the deputy went out there, West wasn't even home. No sign of any trouble. Happened at just about good dark. Six-thirty-seven. Thought you might want to check it out."

"I do," Rhodes said.

He got dressed, looking at his bruises in the bathroom mirror. They were turning a yellowish-green. Kennedy might be old, but he was still plenty strong.

Rhodes took the bandage off the back of his head. The wound probably needed air. He hadn't dreamed, but his sleep had been disturbed several times. Every time he rolled over on his back, the back of his head felt as if he was hitting it on the rock again.

He went into the kitchen and ate a bowl of Quaker Oat Squares for breakfast, thinking that he was turning into a real health-food fanatic. Then he fed Speedo and got ready to drive out to West's store. Speedo wanted to go along, but Rhodes was going in the county car and couldn't take him. To tell the truth, Speedo hadn't proved too useful on his one other foray into investigative work.

West's store looked even less prosperous than it had a couple of days before. Rhodes wondered if there had even been a customer since then. Obviously the signs weren't doing their job of luring buyers.

West was in the store, looking gloomily over the stock, when Rhodes went inside. West looked back at the door hopefully, but the look changed to a frown when he saw Rhodes.

"What can I do for you, Sheriff?" he said. He was wearing his long white apron. "Need some groceries this time?"

"I heard there was some shooting going on out here last night," Rhodes said. "I wondered if you heard it."

"Never heard a thing. I'm a sound sleeper."

"This was early. Six-thirty or so."

"Oh. Well, I was over at Brenda's at six-thirty. Eating supper."

"You didn't mention that you were engaged to her," Rhodes said.

"I thought I did," West said. He stuck his hands beneath his apron and into his jeans pockets. "Does it make any difference?"

"Probably not. You ever get any out-of-season hunting out here, things like that?"

"Nope. I wouldn't worry about those shots, Sheriff, if there were any. My neighbors are mostly old and skittish. It was probably just some kids shooting at mailboxes, or maybe somebody spotlighting rabbits. Maybe somebody's old pickup backfiring."

"I guess you're right," Rhodes said. Things like that weren't uncommon. "It was just something I had to check. I thought maybe Maurice Kennedy had paid you a visit."

"Now why would he want to do that? I'd send him right back to Sunny Dale if I could catch him."

"That might not be as easy as you'd think," Rhodes said.

West looked at the dusty shelves. "Sure I can't sell you some groceries?"

"No, thanks," Rhodes said. "Not today."

At the nursing home, Rhodes said hello to Earlene and went back to Patterson's office. There was a set of dentures on Patterson's desk, sitting on top of a small stack of papers.

Rhodes suddenly remembered a set of plastic teeth someone in his high school class had owned. You wound them up with a key and they chattered and clicked and bounced around. They were supposed to be funny. He didn't think this set would be funny, however.

"Bobbit's?" Rhodes asked, pointing at them before sitting in the hard chair.

"I think they must be Mr. Kennedy's," Patterson said. "They were found in his . . . room."

Rhodes noticed the hesitation. *Here we go again*, he thought, wishing that for once he could get a straight story from somebody. From anybody. "Where in his room?" he asked.

Patterson looked up at the ceiling as if for guidance. Then he looked back down at the desk. "In the plumbing," he said finally, having avoided the indelicate subject for as long as he could.

"You must mean they were found in the toilet," Rhodes said. "I didn't see them in the sink the other day." He hadn't seen them in the toilet, either, for that matter, but they could have been in the pipes. "How did you find them?"

"The room was being cleaned," Patterson said. "When the cleaning woman flushed the toilet, it overflowed. We called a plumber, and he located an obstruction in the line but he couldn't clear it."

Patterson didn't look happy about it, and Rhodes soon found out why. "This was Sunday, of course, and I was paying him double time. He finally had to unseat the toilet and reach into the line. That's where he found the teeth. Don't ask me how they got there. I just don't know. But I suppose Mr. Kennedy could have set them on the back of the commode and knocked them in by accident. If he didn't notice them in there, and then he flushed the toilet, well . . ."

Rhodes could imagine. Kennedy must have lost his own teeth at least two days before Bobbit's death, since that was when Bobbit's teeth had disappeared. Kennedy's dentures then stayed in the pipes long enough to back them up. Rhodes was glad he hadn't been the one to retrieve the teeth.

"You still haven't located Mr. Kennedy, I suppose?" Patterson said.

"No," Rhodes said. "But we're still looking." Ruth had checked the Whataburger that morning, according to Hack. Kennedy had not shown up there. She was checking other places now.

"The poor man. I hope he's staying warm at night."

Patterson's concern was almost touching. It had been another cold night, even colder than before because the cloud cover had disappeared. It had dropped into the upper twenties, according to the report Rhodes had heard Red Rogers giving on the radio that morning. It didn't seem possible that Patterson, who really seemed to care about his residents, could be a killer. Still, Rhodes had to consider every possibility.

"I understand that Sunny Dale is in a little bit of a financial bind," he said.

Patterson looked startled. "Who told you that?"

"A confidential informant. Is it true?"

Patterson reached out and fiddled with the teeth. Then, as if remembering where they'd been, he jerked his hands back. "It's true," he said.

"How bad is it?"

"Not bad," Patterson said, though not very convincingly. "It's more of a cash-flow problem than a bind. You know how it is when there's government red tape involved."

Rhodes didn't know. He said so.

"Many—most—of my guests can't afford the kind of care we provide here. I like to think we do a very good job, and it's expensive. But the government has programs to help out. Sometimes there's difficulty getting the money from the government, and then I have trouble keeping up my payments on the place and meeting my bills. It's nothing that hasn't happened before."

"A hundred thousand dollars would come in pretty handy, though, wouldn't it," Rhodes said.

"Oh, my." Patterson was aghast. "I can see what you're getting at, Sheriff, but I assure you, I would never, ever, kill

141

anyone. Not for a hundred thousand dollars, not for any amount of money. I built Sunny Dale so that I could help people and make their lives easier. I could never do something to hurt one of my guests."

"You did know about Mr. Bobbit's will, though."

"Of course I knew. But I hadn't thought of it since he died. Not until this very minute. I couldn't take advantage of the demise of one of my guests. I just couldn't. I haven't even mentioned the will to Miss Bobbit, since her father died, and I don't intend to. Even if she were to contest the will, I wouldn't care. I didn't want Mr. Bobbit's money."

Rhodes believed him. The man looked shocked at the very suggestion that he might have been involved in Bobbit's death, and Rhodes did not think that Patterson was much of an actor. Nevertheless, he had to ask a few more questions.

"Did you visit Mr. Bobbit's room the day he was killed?"

Patterson started to smooth his hair. Then, as if he remembered having touched the teeth, he jerked his hand down. "I must have," he said. "I visit all my guests nearly every day, if only to say hello. Surely you can't think that I—"

"I don't know what I think, not yet. There are a lot of things about this that bother me."

"But I would never—"

"Don't worry," Rhodes said. "Kennedy is still the best suspect. But until we can find him and question him, we have to keep on investigating."

"I understand," Patterson said, but it was clear that he didn't like it.

Rhodes was sorry about that, but there was nothing that he could do. Until he was certain about who was guilty, he would do what he did best, ask questions, sift the answers, watch the people. Sooner or later, he would know who had murdered Bobbit. He was sure of that.

He changed the subject back to Kennedy, asking about the red jacket.

"Of course," Patterson said. "I should have thought of that. He wore it all the time when he was sitting on the porch. It was reversible, you know."

Rhodes didn't know.

"Yes. Red on one side, black on the other. Quite a nice jacket, really."

Nice, maybe, but the fact that it was reversible was a real pain for Rhodes. It went a long way toward explaining how Kennedy was eluding them. Reverse the jacket, take out the teeth, and Kennedy would look like a different man, given the quality of observation you could usually expect from people these days. Leave the jacket behind, and you'd have a third appearance. It wouldn't be too hard to get by like that for days, even in a town as small as Clearview.

"When's Mr. Bobbit's funeral?" Rhodes asked.

"This afternoon," Patterson said. "Will you be attending?"

"Maybe," Rhodes said.

Mr. West was watching TV again, but not a fishing show. "Jeopardy" was on, and Alex Trebek was reading an answer:

"This young prince avenged the murder of his father at the request of his father's ghost."

"Who was Hamlet?" Rhodes said, just before one of the contestants gave the same question.

West did not move anything but his eyes, shifting them toward the door. "Pretty good, for a sheriff."

Rhodes didn't mention that *Hamlet* was the only Shakespeare play he knew anything about. "How're you feeling today, Mr. West?" he said.

"Same as ever. And that ain't so hot. How about you?"

"I'm fine," Rhodes said, and compared to Mr. West, he was. "I went out for a visit with your son this morning."

"He's a fine boy," West said. He'd said something similar before, but Rhodes detected something ironic in West's tone of voice.

"He's not doing much business at the store," Rhodes said.

West made a motion with his head which Rhodes took for agreement, though it could have been annoyance or even just a meaningless twitch.

"Was a good store, once," West said. "But Obert's not much of a town anymore. Hell, it ain't a town at all. And that road by the store don't go much of anywhere but to Obert."

"It goes on to Stilson," Rhodes said.

"Which ain't much better'n Obert. If that fella gets the college restored, maybe there'll be some traffic out that way. Otherwise, that store might's well close up. Andy's a good boy, but he ain't much of a businessman."

"I understand your son's engaged to Miss Bobbit."

"She's a nice girl," West said. It sounded as if he were trying to convince himself as much as Rhodes.

"Her father had a good deal of money, too," Rhodes said.

"He sure did. Gas money. I always wished they'd strike gas on my land out there by the store, but they never did. It's not even leased now. If Andy marries that girl, he won't have to worry about that, though."

Rhodes got the impression that West thought his son was marrying Miss Bobbit for her money. That was one attraction that Rhodes hadn't thought about, though he should have. Money had the power to make even a cold fish look good.

"I'd like to ask you again about Maurice Kennedy," Rhodes said. "Did you ever talk about Louis Horn, or about the old days in Clearview at all?"

"Not a damn time. He and I didn't associate. I don't think he liked me. He damn sure didn't like Bobbit. Maybe we reminded him too much of those old days."

The conversation wasn't going anywhere. Rhodes glanced back at the TV screen, where a woman was giving the wrong question to the answer, "Her face launched a thousand ships and burnt the topless towers of Ilium."

Rhodes didn't know the answer, either, but he figured it wasn't Brenda Bobbit.

The Stuarts were glad to see Rhodes, and they had already heard about the discovery of the body in the well, as Red Rogers was calling it on his news show. The problems of the jail were already forgotten.

"You think it's Louis Horn, Sheriff?" the Stuarts wanted to know.

Rhodes did, but he told them how hard it would be to prove it. He asked if they had heard any more scuttlebutt around the nursing home.

They had heard about the discovery of the teeth, but that was it.

"That's why I wasn't sure about Kennedy, that day," Mrs. Stuart said. "He was eating just fine, but kind of funny at the same time. I'd probably seen him with his own teeth before, and now that he was using someone else's, he didn't look that different. Just different enough to be worrisome."

"You think you're going to find him, Sheriff?" Mr. Stuart asked.

"Sooner or later," Rhodes said, hoping that it was the truth.

Mr. Bobbit's funeral was sparsely attended. Many of his contemporaries were in Sunny Dale and didn't feel up to being there, and apparently his daughter was not overly supplied with friends who wanted to comfort her. Andy West was there, but he was the only one Rhodes recognized.

Rhodes had come on the off chance that Maurice Kennedy might show up. You never could tell about some people. Unfortunately, Kennedy didn't cooperate. Wherever he was, he stayed there.

The service was mercifully short. The songs were piped in over the sound system, and the minister was brought in on short notice. It was clear that he had no idea just exactly who Mr. Bobbit had been and was merely going through the motions.

Rhodes looked through the visitors' register, but saw no names he was familiar with. He hadn't really expected to see Maurice Kennedy's name, but he thought he would look just in case.

After the service, he went out back to talk to Clyde Ballinger, who was of course fascinated with the discovery of the bones.

"I can see that they're buried, no problem," Ballinger said. "Not like the last time," he added, in reference to a case where a number of anonymous human limbs had turned up in the county. "It would be nice to know who we're burying, though."

"Did Dr. White have any thoughts on that?" Rhodes said, assuming that White would have examined the remains by now.

"All he could say was that the bones belonged to a young male, early twenties, who probably—and I guess it's a big probably—died from a blow on the head. Or several blows."

Rhodes had noticed that the skull was caved in. He thought it might have happened while the body was in the well.

"Might have," Ballinger said. "We'd have to get a real forensic specialist in here, or send the bones off, to find all that out, Dr. White says. Will that be necessary?"

"Maybe not," Rhodes said. "Maybe someone will confess."

"It's Louis Horn," Ballinger said. "Got to be." Ruth had told him the story when she took the bones to the funeral home. "This'd make a great book. Crime from the past, still affecting lives in the present. Real Ross Macdonald stuff."

"Does he work at the 87th precinct?" Rhodes asked.

Ballinger gave him a disgusted look. "Never mind. When are you guys gonna find Maurice Kennedy?"

"I don't know," Rhodes said. He wished people would stop asking him that.

As he was driving away from the funeral home, the radio came to crackling life.

"Godamighty, Sheriff! Godamighty! You there, Sheriff?"

Radio discipline in Blacklin County was so lax as to be almost nonexistent, but even Hack wouldn't go that far.

Rhodes took the mike. "Is that you, Lawton?"

"Yeah, yeah. It's me. Listen, Sheriff, you gotta come to the jail. You gotta come right now!"

"I'm on the way," Rhodes said. At least Lawton knew enough not to give away what was going on to all the scanner listeners in the county. "Where's Hack?"

"He's got a date this afternoon," Lawton said. "With Miz McGee."

Monday was usually a slow day at the jail, and Hack had asked for the afternoon off more than a week before, Rhodes remembered.

"Sheriff, you gotta get here quick," Lawton said. "Billy Joe Bryon's found a dead man in the city dump!"

147

So much for not giving things away, Rhodes thought. He slapped the mike on its hook and stepped on the gas a little harder.

All he needed right now was another dead man.

CHAPTER
FOURTEEN

Billy Joe Bryon had been in the county jail more than once, but not for the purpose of reporting a crime. Rhodes was not quite sure how old Billy Joe was. Probably nobody knew. He'd been around the county ever since anyone could remember, making sort of a living by selling soft drink bottles when they were made of glass and then switching over to aluminum cans, which were going for a little over fifty cents a pound these days.

He had cobbled together a shack out near one of the city's former dump sites—sanitary landfills was the preferred term these days—and he still spent a lot of time combing through the treasures delivered up by the trash trucks at whatever site the city was using at the time. People threw away things that Billy Joe salvaged, some of them still useful, some of them simply junk. He sold whatever he could for whatever he could get. Billy Joe was not of what most people would call "normal intelligence," but he had gotten by without help from the government or anyone else for a long time. He was a common sight in the county, rambling along the side roads, pushing a rusting grocery cart filled with junk and cans.

He was sitting at Rhodes's desk looking at Wanted posters when Rhodes walked in the jail.

Billy Joe jumped up and looked guiltily at the sheriff when the wind ruffled the posters.

"Hey, Billy Joe," Rhodes said. "How're you doing?"

Billy Joe was wearing a pair of ragged overalls, leather work shoes that were cracked near the soles so that his socks showed through, and the remains of two or three flannel shirts. The one on top was red and green. A grayish T-shirt showed at the neck.

"F-f-f-fine," Billy Joe said. "I-I-I-I-"

"He found a dead man at the dump," Lawton said. "It'll take him forever to tell you. I like never to've got it out of him."

The shock of a real crime had done wonders for Lawton's own reluctance to get on with the story. "The trash trucks pick up downtown on Mondays," he said. "Billy Joe likes to be there when they dump so he can sift through and pick out the good stuff. Lord knows what all he finds. Anyhow, the way I get it, he found a body there this morning. Then he walked into town to tell us about it. The 'dozer operator knows about it. He's still there, makin' sure nothin' happens to it."

Billy Joe was looking at Lawton with fascination, his mouth hanging slightly open, as if hearing the story for the first time. Maybe in a way he was.

"Is he telling it right, Billy Joe?" Rhodes said.

Billy Joe swiveled his head to look at Rhodes. "R-r-right."

"Now, this is important, Billy Joe," Rhodes said. "Did the body come from the truck, or was it already there?"

"F-f-from the truck."

"Are you sure?"

"He's sure," Lawton said. "It was all mashed up."

Rhodes thought about the trash trucks. They picked up the dumpsters, which were lifted hydraulically to the top of the container on the back of the truck. When the contents had been emptied into the container, they were compressed with a plunger of some sort so that they wouldn't take up any more space than necessary. It was only natural, then, that the body wouldn't be in very good shape. Rhodes didn't even like to think of what it must look like.

"I guess we'd better get on out there, then, Billy Joe," Rhodes said. "Can you find the body again?"

"I-I-I—"

"He can find it," Lawton said. "He knows right where it is. He told me that already. Besides, the 'dozer operator knows, too."

Billy Joe nodded in agreement.

"All right," Rhodes said. "Come on, Billy Joe. Let's go see what you found. Lawton, you call the Justice of the Peace and an ambulance and tell them to meet us out there."

Even in the winter, Billy Joe smelled a little ripe in the close quarters of the county car. Rhodes figured that Billy Joe's outfit had been assembled sometime around Thanksgiving of last year, before it got to be really cold, and had probably not been removed since.

Rhodes headed for the current dump site, which was just off one of the unpaved county roads to the east of town. Every time the city had to look for a new site, there were complaints from the people who lived nearby. It wasn't so much that they objected to the smell, which could be pretty bad at certain times in the summer; what they really didn't like was the fact that the trucks would be driving up and down the roads near their houses all day, five days a week. So the city tried to find spots in relatively isolated areas of the county if possible.

They had done a pretty good job this time. After Rhodes turned off the pavement, he and Billy Joe passed only one house on the way to the dump. All they saw on either side of them were barbed-wire fences, pastures full of mesquite trees and dead grass, and an occasional cow.

Billy Joe wasn't much of a conversationalist. He sat with his face turned toward the window and watched the passing scenery with just as much fascination as he had looked at Lawton's face in the jail when Lawton was telling about the finding of the body. Anyone who didn't know better might think that Billy Joe had never seen a mesquite tree before in his life.

They came to a break in the fence, with a road leading off to the right. There was a gate, but it was open and pulled back and the chain used to keep it closed was looped around a fence post. There was a sign on the fence that read:

CITY OF CLEARVIEW
SANITARY LANDFILL
You must show your water bill to dump.

Rhodes didn't know whether anyone ever really checked water bills or not. The sign was intended to keep out those who didn't pay city taxes, but he would rather see residents of the county sneak in and dump there than to deposit their trash around in ditches and under bridges as so many of them did.

They drove through the gate and down the caliche road for about two hundred yards. Then they went over a slight rise and they could see the dump.

The theory was that you had a bulldozer dig out huge holes or valleys in the ground. Then you dumped the trash, and the 'dozer pushed it into the hole and covered it up. Eventually, say in four or five hundred years in the case of the plastic rings that held six-packs of beer and sodas together, the trash would biodegrade and be a part of the earth again. Rhodes had heard of cases where the theory didn't pan out, however, and the plastic had somehow

152

worked its way back to the surface of the earth. Tires didn't like to stay down either.

Bodies would biodegrade a lot sooner than tires and plastic, though, and they seldom worked their way out of the ground. Rhodes knew that he was lucky, in a way, that Billy Joe had been at the dump that morning. If the bulldozer had gotten the trash covered, they would most likely never have known about the dead man.

Rhodes stopped the car and he and Billy Joe got out. They could see the bulldozer moving over the hills of trash and hear it chuffing along. Large sections of the ground were bare of grass in places where the 'dozer had already buried trash. The wind blew papers all around—napkins, newspapers, facial tissues, all kinds of papers. There were objects of every description that had been brought to the dump for disposal—bedsprings, mattresses, tires, cans galore, garbage, everything imaginable—and all were waiting to be bulldozed under.

"You sure the 'dozer operator knew about the dead man?" Rhodes said.

"S-s-s-sure," Billy Joe said.

"All right," Rhodes said. "Show me where he is." He assumed that the 'dozer operator had to get on with his work, no matter whether a gruesome discovery had been made at the dump. Keeping up with the rising piles of garbage and trash was a full-time job.

Billy Joe led Rhodes over to a pile of trash that hadn't been touched by the 'dozer.

There was no question that what was lying on one side of the pile was something that had once been a man. Rhodes couldn't tell much about his face, but he recognized the red coat. They would have to check the teeth to be sure, but it looked as if he had found Maurice Kennedy.

"Jesus, I never saw anything like that, Sheriff," Clyde Ballinger said. "You've sent some strange things my

153

way before, but this one takes the cake. He was really mashed up."

"Yes," Rhodes said. "He was." He'd never seen anything like it, himself, and he didn't care if he never did again. Billy Joe didn't seem particularly bothered, for some reason, and Rhodes guessed he'd seen some pretty weird things at the dump over the years.

But Rhodes hadn't. It looked as if most of Kennedy's bones were broken, his mashed and bloody face was unrecognizable, and Rhodes just hoped the teeth were intact. He hadn't tried to find out. He hadn't even looked for his pistol, but Billy Joe had pointed it out. It was sticking out of the pocket of the reversible jacket, and Rhodes had retrieved it. It was now lying in the floor of the county car.

"How in the world did he get in that dumpster?" Ballinger asked.

Rhodes had been thinking about that. "Maybe he climbed in," he said.

"Climbed in? What for?"

"To keep warm." The way Rhodes saw it, that was how Kennedy had been eluding them. Who would think of looking in a dumpster? It was a place to stay out of the cold, and if you pulled some newspapers or cardboard around you, you could survive the night easily enough. Newspapers and cardboard were in plentiful supply in dumpsters. It wouldn't be comfortable, but you could stand it. From what Rhodes had heard, there were people on the streets of Houston who got through the whole winter with less.

"Maybe," Ballinger said when Rhodes told him his theory. "But why didn't he wake up when the truck was picking him up? You'd think he'd scream and take on like anything. I know I would."

Rhodes had a theory about that, too. In fact, he had two theories. One was that the truck was making so much noise

154

that the workers inside, who would have had the windows rolled up, the heater fan on, and the radio turned up loud and tuned to some station that played rap songs, could not hear Kennedy's yells. Kennedy, being old, and, despite his prowess with a tree limb, none too agile, would not have been able to get out of the dumpster in time to save himself.

The other theory was that Kennedy might have been drinking to keep himself warm. The fact that alcohol didn't really work like that probably wouldn't have bothered him. If he'd drunk enough, he might never have known what was happening to him.

Rhodes hoped the second theory was the correct one, even if Kennedy probably was guilty of having killed two men. The thought of him being aware and awake while he was being crushed was just too much, no matter what his past crimes were.

"Dr. White ought to be able to tell you if he'd been drinking," Ballinger said. "There's enough blood left in him for that. Boy, he was sure a mess, though."

Rhodes wondered if Ballinger was thinking of Kennedy as a challenge to his professional abilities. Probably not. No one would much care if there was a closed casket at the funeral. There might not even be anyone there to notice.

"I guess you're glad to have all this wrapped up," Ballinger said. "The boys at the eight-seven couldn't have done it any better."

"I didn't do anything," Rhodes said.

"Doesn't matter. Folks will give you the credit. Two murders cleared up, one of 'em more than fifty years old. You'll be a hero."

Rhodes didn't feel like a hero. He just felt tired and sore. But no matter how sore he was, Kennedy was in much worse shape. Getting whipped up on with a tree limb was nothing compared to getting mashed to death. The only good thing about finding Kennedy, as far as Rhodes was concerned, was that he could close the cases and worry about the lawsuit. And about getting married.

He went back to the jail to write his reports. Hack and Mrs. McGee were there, along with Lawton.

Mrs. McGee didn't like the cold. She was wearing a knit cap which she had pulled down over her forehead, completely covering her hair. She was wearing a puffy ski jacket like Mr. Bobbit's, except that hers was green, and she had on a pair of wool pants that looked as if they might have belonged to her late husband. She was also wearing a pair of galoshes with buckles up the front. Rhodes hadn't seen galoshes like that in years. She was much shorter than Hack, who was tall and thin. Mrs. McGee was more Lawton's size, though not quite as chubby, and certainly not as smooth-faced.

"You boys have a lot goin' on all the time," she said when Rhodes came in the door. "Lawton here was just tellin' us about the man at the dump."

"Who was it, Sheriff?" Lawton asked. Rhodes could tell that he was feeling really good, because for one of the first times in years he had most of the lowdown on a story that Hack had missed out on. Rhodes wondered how long it had taken him to tell everything to Hack and Mrs. McGee.

"I haven't established the identity yet," Rhodes said. "Dr. White is going to have the dentures checked. But I'm pretty sure it's Maurice Kennedy."

Hack and Lawton took the news about the same way Ballinger had. They were sure the Sheriff's Department would get credit for finding Kennedy, which would show how efficient the operation was and take the heat off the lawsuit. They weren't particularly sorry for Kennedy, either.

Neither was Mrs. McGee. "Got exactly what he deserved, the old scoundrel," she said. "Anybody that'd take a man's teeth, well, he'd do just about anything. I just know he killed that Louis Horn."

It didn't really matter whether he had or not, though Rhodes agreed with Mrs. McGee on that point, and it didn't really matter whose bones they had uncovered at the Old Settlers' Grounds, either, though Rhodes was confident that they were Horn's. Rhodes was sure they could close the Horn case now and that everyone would be happy. For some reason, however, he still wasn't so sure about the death of Mr. Bobbit.

"Where did you two go this afternoon?" he asked Mrs. McGee.

"To the movies," Hack said.

Clearview still had a theater, although it had fallen on hard times. It charged an admission of one dollar in the evenings and fifty cents in the afternoons. It showed mostly films that were about a week away from being released on video cassettes, which were the things that had just about killed its business. The only advantage in going there was that you could at least see the movie on a big screen. Even that was not as good as it sounded, since the prints the theater received were often scratchy, poorly spliced, and so dark that you could hardly make out the actors.

"What did you see?" he asked.

"*Batman*," Hack said. "Now there's a guy knows how to fight crime."

"Hack's right," Mrs. McGee said. "If you had that Batmobile, Sheriff, you wouldn't have any trouble with criminals in this town at all."

Rhodes was afraid he wouldn't even be able to drive the Batmobile, much less operate its complicated weapons system. And he wondered just how much good it would do him in the case of stolen dentures. Batman had more serious things to occupy his time.

Hack and Mrs. McGee left to go somewhere for a burger. It occurred to Rhodes that he had missed lunch again, and he bribed Lawton to go over to the court house for a couple of bottled Dr Peppers.

He spent the rest of the afternoon writing his reports and wondering if Ivy was going to talk to him that night.

Ivy was indeed willing to talk. She seemed to have gotten over any hard feelings she had against Rhodes for getting himself beaten nearly to a pulp, and she was glad that Maurice Kennedy had been found and dealt with. She admitted, however, that it seemed a pretty horrible way to go.

"Have you told Mr. Patterson?" she asked.

"I gave him a call this afternoon. He was sorry to hear it, I think. No matter what Kennedy did, he was still one of the 'guests' to Mr. Patterson."

"What about Miss Bobbit?"

"I thought I ought to tell her in person," Rhodes said. "I thought you and I could go out for supper, maybe to the Jolly Tamale, and I could go by her house on the way out there."

It sounded like a good idea to Ivy. They would be able to ride in the county car since they were on official business; the only drawback from Ivy's point of view was that there was no reason to use the siren.

When she got in the car, her foot kicked the pistol Rhodes had put there earlier.

"What's that?" she said.

Rhodes reached around her and picked up the gun. "It was on Kennedy's body," he explained. "I was going to clean it, but I forgot all about it."

"I'm sorry I touched it," Ivy said.

"It was in his jacket," Rhodes said. "I don't think it got too bloody."

"Just the same . . ."

Rhodes opened the back door and put the pistol on the floor. He would clean it in the morning. A cursory glance at it that afternoon seemed to indicate that it hadn't been harmed by being compacted along with Kennedy. Rhodes didn't like to think about how it had been cushioned or about what he might find when he cleaned it. But it was a good gun. He would have to take care of it sooner or later.

Later seemed better, this time.

FIFTEEN

Ivy waited in the car while Rhodes went up to Miss Bobbit's house. There was another car parked in front, a dilapidated Ford about ten years old, and Rhodes wasn't surprised to find that Andy West was inside when Miss Bobbit answered the door. She asked Rhodes to come in, and he entered the foyer.

"I just wanted to come by and tell you that we found Mr. Kennedy today," Rhodes said.

She looked surprised and glanced back over her shoulder. West was sitting on the couch. He got up and walked over to the door. It was the first time Rhodes had seen him without his apron on. He looked pretty much the same except that he was scowling even more than usual.

"Is this gonna cause us any more problems?" he said. He was clearly agitated about something.

"I was just telling Andy that we might have to delay our marriage," Miss Bobbit explained to Rhodes.

"Why is it that the law always has to complicate things?" West said. He turned to Miss Bobbit. "I wish I'd known about that power of attorney."

"I . . . why, it never seemed important," Miss Bobbit

said. "I never knew that it ended with death. I guess Mr. Dunstable told me, but I don't remember. Anyway, probate won't take too long. Mr. Dunstable has assured me that there won't be any problems. Finding Mr. Kennedy won't change that." She looked at Rhodes, her eyes hidden by the glasses. "He's in jail, I hope."

"No," Rhodes said. "He's not in jail."

"But you said—"

"I said we found him. I didn't say he was alive." It was totally inappropriate, but Rhodes found himself thinking he sounded like Hack and Lawton.

"Oh. You mean—"

"He's dead."

"Nothing wrong with that," West said. "Just make things easier for us, I bet."

He was right about that, Rhodes supposed. There wouldn't be any ongoing investigation to interfere with the probate process.

"What happened to the old guy, Sheriff?" West asked.

Rhodes told them.

"Heck of a way to go," West said, but he didn't seem too concerned about it. It was clear that the main thing he wanted was to make sure there were no impediments to his marriage.

"Did he have the . . . the teeth?" Miss Bobbit said.

"He had dentures," Rhodes said, remembering Kennedy's crushed head. "We're not sure yet whose they were, but Dr. White will have given them to the dentist by now. We'll know tomorrow."

"Well, I guess that settles that, then," West said. "He took the teeth and killed Lloyd. It's a damn shame."

Miss Bobbit didn't seem to think it was a shame. She didn't seem very upset by the two deaths. "There won't be any more publicity about all this, will there?" she asked.

"It's not every day we find a body in the city dump," Rhodes said. "I'd say this will be a front-page story."

"But my name won't be involved, will it?"

"Maybe not," Rhodes said. "Not too much, anyway." Most of the story would concern the discovery of the body in the dump, the sensational part, if he knew how newspapers worked. Billy Joe Bryon would make good copy, too. The colorful local character. The newspaper would want to run a picture of his house. Maybe Red Rogers would even try to interview him. Rhodes would like to hear that one. And of course there would be a lot about Kennedy's connection with the Body in the Well. The Bobbits would most likely be just a footnote.

Miss Bobbit seemed relieved. Rhodes left her there with her fiancé and went back to the car. They seemed to him to be a strange couple. He and Ivy were pretty normal by comparison, or at least he liked to think so.

"How did she take the news?" Ivy asked when he was back in the car.

"She was glad to hear it, I guess. With her, it's hard to tell. She's glad it's over, though."

Ivy smiled. "Well, King, this case is closed," she said.

"Thank you, Sergeant Preston," Rhodes said.

At the Jolly Tamale, Rhodes and Ivy had chicken fajitas for two, with side dishes of beans and rice. Guacamole, pico de gallo, cheese, and sour cream were provided to garnish the chicken, which they rolled in flour tortillas along with grilled onions and green peppers. They also had tortilla chips to eat with the red sauce on the table. Rhodes washed it all down with Dr Pepper, though Ivy stuck to iced tea.

After he had finished eating, Rhodes suspected that he knew why he was gaining weight even when he skipped lunch. He was afraid he might have to loosen his belt buckle to get out of the restaurant.

They drove back to Rhodes's house, and Ivy insisted on

163

going around to the back yard to greet Speedo. Speedo was glad to see both of them, frolicking around the yard, barking and running, and Rhodes felt guilty that he didn't have more time to spend with his dog.

When they went in the house, the phone was ringing.

Rhodes picked it up and answered. It was his daughter, Kathy.

"Hi, Dad," she said. She sounded well and happy, for which Rhodes was grateful. She was twenty-four years old, teaching school near Dallas, but Rhodes still worried about her.

"Hi, yourself," he said. "What's going on?"

"I was wondering about the big wedding," she said. "Is it still on for Friday?"

"You'd better ask Ivy about that. She's right here."

"Let me talk to her then."

Rhodes handed Ivy the phone. She listened for a few seconds, then laughed, looking at Rhodes.

"Yes," she said. "It's still on."

She listened again.

"I *hope* he sounded worried," she said. "I did get a little upset with him, but I got over it. . . . No, it wasn't anything he did to me. He's usually very sweet."

She looked at Rhodes, who felt his ears getting warm. He didn't like to hear himself talked about that way, not even if it was to his daughter.

"What?" Ivy said into the phone. "No, it was nothing like that. It was just something that happened. It's bothered me before, and I know I should be used to it by now, but it's not easy. . . . Yes, I'm sure you worry about him, too."

Rhodes didn't like to hear that, either. He was supposed to be the one who did the worrying in the family. Other people weren't supposed to be worrying about him.

"I'll tell you about it Friday," Ivy was saying. "He

probably wouldn't even mention it, but it's a pretty good story."

She listened some more, said she'd see Kathy on Friday, and handed the phone back to Rhodes.

"What have you been up to?" Kathy asked.

"Nothing very exciting. Did I hear Ivy say something about seeing you on Friday?"

"You didn't think I'd miss the wedding, did you? I'm taking a personal business day to be there."

"We're just going to be married by the county judge," Rhodes said. "It won't be a big deal. Won't take more than five minutes."

"You incurable romantic, you," Kathy said. "I'm not going to miss it, even if it does take just five minutes. It's not every day a woman's father gets married."

"What about you?" Rhodes said. Kathy had once dated a deputy on Rhodes's staff, and she had left Clearview shortly after that romance had ended unhappily. Or not. Rhodes supposed it all depended on your point of view.

"You might be getting a surprise on Friday," she said. "There's someone I'd like for you to meet."

"What's his name?"

"Greg," Kathy said. "He teaches math. What time will you be getting married?"

Rhodes hadn't really thought about that. He realized suddenly that he was being entirely too casual about the whole thing, and he thought that might be an unspoken reason why Ivy had been upset with him. He didn't blame her. He'd more or less thought he'd wait until he got a few spare minutes, call Ivy, and walk over to the court house. He knew now that wouldn't be a good idea.

"Eleven o'clock," he said.

"Good. I can get there easily by that time. I'll see you then. I love you."

"I love you, too," Rhodes said. Then he hung up the phone.

"Eleven o'clock, huh?" Ivy said.

"Will that be all right with you?"

"I suppose so. And what will we be doing after our five minutes are up?"

There was no edge to her voice, but Rhodes was beginning to realize that no matter what Ivy had said to Kathy, he was guilty of a mistake much worse than that of allowing an old man to beat him with a tree limb.

He was guilty of taking Ivy for granted. Not only had he not talked with her about the housing situation, he hadn't even set a time for the wedding. Ivy might have thought she was angry with him for putting himself in danger, but that wasn't the only reason. No wonder she had been upset. He was an insensitive creep.

Why, he had never even considered what they would be doing after they got married. He and his first wife had gone to Colorado on their honeymoon. They had driven through New Mexico, through Raton Pass, and on up to Colorado Springs. They had stayed in the Broadmoor Hotel for two days, which was all they could afford, and then they had driven back to Texas.

"Have you ever been to Cozumel?" he said. He had heard that it was a beautiful place, and he'd seen ads for it on TV. He'd never been there himself.

"No," Ivy said. "Were you planning to take me?"

Rhodes figured that planning could consist of ten seconds thought if you didn't put too strict a limitation on the meaning.

"Yes," he said, wondering if the local travel agency would be able to get them a flight and book them into a hotel on short notice. He didn't know what the tourist season was in Cozumel, but he thought there might be a lot of people going there to keep warm in the winter. Maybe he had enough pull with someone in the travel agency to work something out. He'd have to see about it first thing in the morning.

166

"You believe in keeping things to yourself, don't you?"

Ivy did not sound unduly suspicious. Rhodes knew that he was somewhat reticent, a quality that usually served him well in his work. It wasn't going to serve him well in marriage, though it might have gotten him out of this situation. It was something he'd have to work on.

"I'll try to do better," he said.

"It's always nice to be surprised," Ivy said. "But you should have let me know sooner. I need to buy a bathing suit and some summer clothes." She looked distressed. "I don't know where I can find anything at this time of year."

"Well," Rhodes said, thinking that he might have an out, "I can cancel if you'd rather just go somewhere close. We could drive down to Houston and spend a few days."

"Oh, no. I think Cozumel would be wonderful. I've got an old suit that doesn't look too out of style. Of course it doesn't show as much as those new ones do."

Rhodes thought about some photos he had seen in last spring's *Sports Illustrated* swimsuit issue that someone had left in the jail. He was just as glad Ivy wouldn't be wearing anything that revealing. He was sure she would look great, but he was a little too old-fashioned to feel comfortable with a suit that exposed almost all of a woman's anatomy.

"I'm not sure I can take the time off, anyway," he said. "What with these murders and Kennedy turning up dead—"

"How long has it been since you had a day off?" Ivy said. "One year? Two? Five?"

Rhodes thought about it. Since his wife had died, he had pretty much devoted himself to the job. Kathy had lived with him for a while, but then she had seen she wasn't needed anymore and moved away after breaking up with the deputy. He didn't have anyone except Speedo to go on a trip with him and nowhere to go except home and the jail. He knew that he had not taken any time off, not even a day, for a long time.

"It's been a while," he admitted.

"So it's about time. You're not going to get out of this now. No one would dare object to your taking a short trip. When are we leaving?"

He wondered how much extra time he could buy. Not much. But even a day might make a difference in getting the tickets.

"Uh, Saturday," he said. "I thought we'd drive to Dallas, stay there Friday night, fly out on Saturday."

Ivy was getting excited. "That's wonderful. I'll need to pack, but that won't take long. Some of the stores may already have their summer things in. The spring outfits are already on the racks. I'll go shopping tomorrow at lunch."

"Uh, are you sure you can get off?"

"I've already asked for my two weeks' vacation. That won't be a problem."

"Great," Rhodes said. He felt like a criminal, himself. He hoped he knew someone at the travel agency, and for a minute he wished that Billy Joe Bryon had never left home today. If he hadn't found Kennedy's body, then Rhodes would have had a perfect excuse to put things off. As it was, he was going to have to produce. Then he dismissed his regrets as unworthy. He could take care of things. There would be no problem. He told himself that two or three times, and eventually he even started to believe it.

They decided to watch TV for a while before Ivy went home, and that was when Rhodes discovered that things were never so bad they couldn't get even worse.

"I can't read this *TV Guide*," he said, flipping through the pages. "Is the light bulb all right?"

"The light's fine," Ivy said. "Here. Let me have that."

Rhodes handed her the magazine. "There's nothing wrong with the print," Ivy said. "I can see it just fine. The late movie is *The Red Badge of Courage*. You like Audie Murphy, don't you?"

"Yes," Rhodes said. He had read an article about Murphy in an issue of *Texas Monthly* some time ago. The article had been excerpted from a biography of Murphy written by someone named Don Graham. Rhodes had been intending to buy the book, but he never had much time to read. Watching old movies didn't require as much concentration. Now he was wondering if he would be able to read the book if he bought it. He could still see the movies just fine, however.

"Let me see that magazine," he said.

Ivy handed it back. He still could not read the program description. He carried the magazine to a lamp and turned on the light. Holding the *TV Guide* at arm's length and getting it fully under the light, he was able to see what the anonymous critic had to say about the movie.

"Did you ever think about getting reading glasses?" Ivy said. "You can buy them at the drug store."

"I thought about it," Rhodes admitted. "I just haven't had time."

"There are a few other things you need to find time for, too."

"What?" Rhodes wondered just exactly what he'd forgotten now.

"A blood test, for one thing," Ivy said. "Not to mention a little detail like the marriage license. You'd better take care of your blood test tomorrow, so the doctor will have time to get the lab work done. I've had mine done already. And it wouldn't hurt to get the license soon, either."

"That's what I was planning to do," Rhodes said, stretching the definition of "planning" just about as far as it could be stretched.

"Good," Ivy said. "I was afraid that with all the excitement, you might forget."

"I won't forget," Rhodes promised.

CHAPTER

SIXTEEN

Having promised, Rhodes did not forget, but he almost got sidetracked. He had other things to do first, including making a stop at Wal-Mart, where he thought he'd seen reading glasses on a rack near the jewelry counter.

He had, and he tried on several of the half-moon type before settling on a gray pair with the number 1.25 on the tag. He supposed that meant everything he saw through them would be magnified one and one-fourth normal size.

He was amazed at how well he could read the print on the display with the glasses on. They had the unfortunate effect of making him look like Ben Franklin with a belly-ache, or so he thought when he glimpsed himself in the mirror above the rack. But that was better than not being able to read the *TV Guide*, so he paid for the glasses. He took them out of the bag when he got outside and slipped them in his shirt pocket.

Then he went by the travel agency, where he discovered one of the agents to be Lacey Hollowell, a young woman who had gone to school with Kathy. It wasn't easy, but Lacey managed to get him and Ivy a Saturday flight out of

Dallas and a room at one of the better hotels in Cozumel, thanks to a last minute cancellation by someone or other whom Rhodes would never meet but to whom he would be eternally in debt. He paid with his Visa card, thankful that things had worked out. Before he signed the Visa slip, he put on his glasses and was pleased that he had no difficulty seeing the little space where he was to write his name.

He went by the jail on his way to the doctor's office for the blood test, and he was almost sorry that he stopped. The jail was where the major distractions were.

For one thing, Hack and Lawton had big news. It had nothing to do with Lloyd Bobbit or Maurice Kennedy—that was yesterday's case, and closed up tighter than Dick's hat band, as Hack liked to put it. Kennedy was dead, the murders were solved, and everyone was happy. This was something entirely different.

Hack started things off. "We had us a real problem last night," he said.

Rhodes decided to get his licks while he could. "Was Miz McGee in on this, or had you taken her home?"

Lawton found that remark particularly funny. He laughed so hard that his smooth, chubby face got extremely red and he sounded as if he might choke.

"What's the matter with him?" Rhodes said.

"It's that girl we had in here last night," Hack said.

"The real problem was a girl?" Rhodes asked.

"That's what I was trying to tell you," Hack said, though Rhodes didn't think he'd been trying very hard.

"It's a g-g-good thing Miz McGee was g-g-gone," Lawton said. Then he was overcome by laughter again, and this time he laughed so hard that he started coughing. Rhodes resisted the urge to walk across the office and pound him on the back.

"Tell me about the girl," Rhodes said. He was getting curious and thought maybe the direct approach would be the best.

"She fell out of a car," Hack said, and Rhodes knew that the direct approach had failed again. There was nothing very funny about falling out of a car.

"Was she hurt?" he said. He knew that she hadn't been; he would have been called in that case, and there wouldn't have been such an excess of joviality in the office.

"Naw, she wasn't hurt bad," Hack said. "The car wasn't goin' very fast when she fell out."

"*Part* of her was hurt," Lawton said, having gotten his breath. "Gonna take the doctor a good while to pick all that gravel out."

"What gravel? Out of where?" Rhodes said.

"The gravel in her behind," Hack said. "She couldn't even sit down when she was in here."

What Rhodes wanted to know, naturally, was exactly how the gravel had gotten embedded in the girl's delicate anatomy, but he was determined not to ask.

"Was she the driver of the car?" he said.

Lawton started laughing again, but Hack was able to maintain a straight face through it all. They often reminded Rhodes of Abbott and Costello, but never more than at times like this. He almost found himself asking them who was on third base.

"Couldn't have been drivin', not the way she was when she fell out," Hack said.

Rhodes was beginning to catch on. "She didn't have any clothes on, did she."

"Sure she did," Hack said. "You don't think any of Blacklin County's young ladies would drive around without any clothes on a-tall, do you?"

Rhodes said he wasn't sure *what* Blacklin County's young ladies might do these days.

"Well, anyway," Hack said, "she had her clothes on."

"Mostly," Lawton said, giving the game away. Hack turned and gave him a look that would have sanded the

173

paint off a county car. He had obviously hoped to keep things going for a while longer.

"She fell out of the car while she was mooning someone," Rhodes said. Some of the kids thought it was funny to give the adults a shock every now and then; it had been happening fairly often lately.

"That's right," Hack said, obviously not too happy that Rhodes had figured it out so soon. "Mooned the wrong person this time, though."

"Buddy?" Rhodes said. Buddy had been one of the deputies on duty last night, and he was a strict, old-fashioned moralist, sort of along the lines of Cotton Mather.

"Yeah, it was Buddy," Hack said. Rhodes had taken all the fun out of things by putting it together, and Hack was ready to tell the whole story. "Buddy'd stopped a drunk driver at the edge of town and he was talkin' to him, tryin' to get him out of the car. It was pretty late, about two o'clock. Buddy followed the car for nearly a mile he said, with it weavin' all over the place."

"Guy didn't want to get out," Lawton chimed in. "He figured he was too drunk to stand up and that wouldn't look good to the judge when Buddy told it in court, so he was just sittin' there behind the wheel. Singin' 'The Whiffenpoof Song' off-key Buddy said. I don't think I know that one, do you, Sheriff?"

Rhodes said that he did, but that he wasn't going to sing any of it right then.

"You could sing it off-key," Lawton said. "If Buddy can stand it, I can."

Rhodes said he'd rather hear what happened.

"Well," Hack said, "Buddy was there by the car and these girls drove by. Goin' real slow, Buddy said. He looked up, like anybody would, and the one on the passenger side mooned him. Might've got away, since he didn't want to leave the drunk, if the door hadn't come open."

174

"Musta got her pants hung on the door handle," Lawton said. "It was an old car. They don't make handles where you can get stuff hung on 'em these days."

"Fell right on her butt," Hack said. "Slid a good little ways on the road. That's where she picked up the gravel."

"Buddy arrested the whole bunch of 'em," Lawton said. "The drunk, the girls in the car, all of 'em. Brought 'em down here for me to book 'em. It was real noisy for a while, what with the way the girl was cryin'. The drunk guy had switched to 'My Way.' I know that one, though."

"Then he stopped singin' and started hollerin' for the girl to show us the evidence," Hack said.

"Did she?" Rhodes asked.

"Naw," Lawton said. "She had her clothes on by then, but it's just as well Miz McGee wasn't here. That sure was a cute little ol' gal. Prob'ly not more'n nineteen. Miz McGee wouldn't like it if Hack was to see somethin' like that."

He started laughing again. He seemed to find something inherently humorous in Hack's romance. Hack watched him, stony-faced.

"Anybody still here?" Rhodes asked.

"The drunk is," Hack said. "Upstairs sleepin' it off. Buddy didn't put the girls in a cell, but he sure wanted to do it. He wanted to send 'em up the river."

Rhodes believed it. Buddy was not only a strict moralist; his sense of humor was more akin to Jerry Falwell's than Jerry Lewis's.

"We talked him out of it, finally," Lawton said. "I didn't much like the idea of keepin' three girls in jail overnight. Besides, that one with the rear-end trouble needed to go by the hospital."

"I'm glad you talked him out of jailing them," Rhodes said. He figured they'd been punished enough, or at least one of them had. She wouldn't want to be seen in one of those new bathing suits even by the time summer rolled

175

around. He hoped she really had gone to the hospital and gotten the gravel taken care of.

"I guess Buddy did give them a ticket, though," he said.

"Darn right, he did," Hack said. "More'n one, if I remember right. They said they'd appear before the Justice of the Peace and pay up."

That seemed to be the extent of what there was to say on the subject, and Rhodes was looking at some of the other reports from the previous evening, none of them as interesting as the one Hack and Lawton had provided, when he realized that he couldn't make out the reports very well. He slipped the glasses out of his pocket as unobtrusively as he could, unfolded the sidepieces, and put them on.

Hack noticed immediately. "What you got there?" he said. "New pair of cheaters?"

Rhodes looked at him without saying anything, peering over the top of the glasses.

"You look kinda mean like that," Hack said, and then he turned back to his desk. He didn't have anything else to add.

Lawton smiled, but he didn't say anything.

Rhodes turned back to the reports and kept on reading, finding it much easier with the glasses on. They were uncomfortable sitting there on the bridge of his nose, and the sidepieces hurt his ears, but the discomfort was worth it. Being able to see the reports so clearly made him realize how long he'd been needing the glasses. He was going to have to stop putting things like that off.

He had been reading for about a half hour when James Allen entered the jail. Rhodes slipped the glasses off his face and back into his pocket. No need in letting Allen see them. The commissioner might think the county sheriff was getting old.

"You were right," Allen told Rhodes after greeting Hack and Lawton.

"Good," Rhodes said. "What was I right about?"

"That rain. I sent Miz Wilkie over to the newspaper office to check the weather records. It didn't rain a single drop while you had Little Barnes in jail."

"I guess that's good news," Rhodes said. "What about those structural engineers? Is that going to get us the rest of the way off the hook?"

"Maybe. That lawyer's already started waffling. I called him this morning and dropped him a hint about the rain, said I thought that tainted his whole case. Then I told him we were gonna have that outside firm come in and do a study of the jail. Took some of the wind out of his sails."

"How much wind?"

"What I think is, he'll try for a small settlement. But we might not even have to worry about that. I found out that Harry Harmon is the presiding district judge, and he'd be the one to hear the case."

"Hanging Harry," Rhodes said.

Allen smiled a satisfied smile. "The very same."

Hanging Harry was a man who had achieved his present position by his hard-line approach to law and order. District judges in Texas were elected, and Harry Harmon had swept in on his record as a county prosecutor who seldom lost a case and who *never* lost a major case.

He got sentences that other prosecutors could only dream of, and had once gotten a small-time drug dealer— which was the only kind that Blacklin county had—a sentence exceeding a hundred years. Since becoming a judge, he had handed down some sentences that made that one seem light. There wasn't a criminal in the state that wanted to come up before him. Harmon might have been many things, but he was definitely not soft on crime.

Not even a hot-shot attorney from Houston would want Harmon sitting on a case where a convicted criminal was complaining about his treatment in a county jail. Harmon's expressed opinion was that the best thing the state could do to cut the crime rate would be to bring back the rack and the thumbscrew.

"That sounds good," Rhodes said. "When are those engineers going to be here?"

"Friday," Allen said.

It took a lot of talking to convince Allen that the sheriff didn't necessarily have to be there when the engineers made their inspection of the jail.

"I know you're getting married," Allen said. "And I can see that it's going to be a problem. I guess Miz Wilkie just forgot what day it was when she scheduled the visit."

Rhodes thought he heard Hack snort, but when he looked over at him, the dispatcher was busily writing something on a note pad. Lawton was sitting at Hack's desk, looking down as if studying the pattern of cracks in the floor and trying to hide a smile.

"I can't be here," Rhodes said. "There's just no way. I've got airplane tickets to Mexico."

Rhodes heard Hack's chair creak as the dispatcher turned around. He and Lawton gave up all pretense of being involved with their own concerns. They both turned toward Rhodes's desk with unabashed interest. Rhodes thought it served them right. If they hadn't started up about the mooning incident and dragged it out like they had, he would have told them about the trip to Cozumel. He still would, sooner or later, but he knew they wouldn't like it because Allen was finding out first.

"Cozumel," Rhodes said. "Ever been there?"

Allen had not, though he had been to the Virgin Islands. "You gonna do any snorkeling?"

Rhodes thought not. "But I'm going. No question about that." He didn't mention that he was afraid Ivy would kill him if he tried backing out of the trip.

Allen finally agreed that it was only right that Rhodes

be allowed a little time off since he was getting married and since he hadn't taken any vacation time in years.

Rhodes assured the commissioner that Hack and Lawton could take care of the engineers. Maybe if he praised them enough, they would forgive him for not telling them about the trip to Mexico.

They weren't interested in praise, however. After Allen left, Hack asked Lawton what he had in the pool.

"Cancun. I was pretty close. How about you?"

"Belize," Hack said.

"Wait just a minute," Rhodes said. "I know there was a pool on the wedding date, but you don't mean to tell me there was one on the honeymoon, too."

"Sure there was," Hack said. "Me and Lawton were beginnin' to wonder if you were ever goin' to get around to thinkin' about takin' one, though. You have any trouble gettin' the tickets?"

"No," Rhodes said. "I've been planning it for a long time."

"Sure you had," Lawton said. "A man likes to plan ahead."

He went to clean the cells. He said that if the drunk was up, he was going to try to get him to sing "The Whiffenpoof Song." This time it was Hack who was laughing.

The blood test was the last of the day's little chores, and the least pleasant. It wasn't that Rhodes got weak or queasy at the sight of blood, though it was something he never got used to; it was just that he didn't like the idea of getting stuck with the needle.

He told himself that was a silly way to be and that a man with spectacular bruises on his back and chest, not to mention a few stitches on the back of his head, shouldn't be intimidated by a small woman with a needle.

179

He was intimidated anyway, but he managed not to flinch when she stuck it in him.

After he left the doctor's office, he drove by Ballinger's to see if Dr. White had left a report on his autopsy of Maurice Kennedy. He also wanted to see if the dentist had called about the teeth.

Ballinger was glad to see him. "You sure do know how to complicate things," he said when Rhodes walked in his office.

There was a book lying face down on the desk, its spine in the air. Rhodes sneaked a glance at the cover. It was called *Drive East on 66*, by someone named Richard Wormser. He could see the cover easily; he was far enough away from it not to need his glasses.

Ballinger caught the glance. "It's an old one, all right. I don't think anybody drives on Sixty-six anymore. There used to be a TV show about that highway, about those two guys in a Corvette, but I don't even know if it's still there. There was even a song."

"It's still there," Rhodes said. "What's this about me knowing how to complicate things."

"You know that old boy you brought in here yesterday, that Maurice Kennedy?"

"I know," Rhodes said. "That's why I came by, to ask about him."

"Well, in the first place we got the word from Dr. Richards about a half hour ago. Those were Lloyd Bobbit's dentures Mr. Kennedy was wearing. Dr. Richards would be willing to swear to that in court if he has to."

"He probably won't have to," Rhodes said, glad to know that everyone's suspicions about the dentures had been confirmed. "I don't think even Miss Bobbit will be filing a complaint against a dead man."

"No, I don't guess so," Ballinger said. "Wouldn't do a whole lot of good, would it."

"No," Rhodes said. "It wouldn't. We pretty well knew

180

about the teeth all along, though. What's the complication?"

"Oh," Ballinger said. "That. Well, you know how when you heard where the body came from and all, you thought Kennedy'd been mashed to death by the trash truck?"

"That's what I thought," Rhodes said. "You saw him, too."

"I sure did. And I thought the same thing. Anybody would, considering the way he looked and that Billy Joe saw him dumped out of the truck along with the trash."

"You sound like that wasn't what happened," Rhodes said, feeling a little ball of apprehension beginning to form in his stomach.

"It wasn't," Ballinger said. "It was something else entirely." He looked thoughtful. "Or maybe not entirely. He'd been mashed up, all right. If you hadn't had Dr. White look at the body, we probably wouldn't ever have known that it wasn't the trash truck that killed him."

"What did kill him then?" Rhodes asked. He didn't like the way this was going.

"I can't tell you that. Neither can Dr. White, but he can come close. He said it was a blow to the back of the head with a blunt instrument."

"But it wasn't the trash truck."

"Nope. Like I said, you'd never notice it. The body was in pretty bad shape. The head, too. But according to Dr. White, the way the back of Kennedy's skull was caved in wasn't consistent with the way the trash truck operates. It wasn't just mashed. It was splintered in, the way it'd have to be if somebody hit it with something. Like a wrench, maybe. Hit it hard. You know what I mean?"

Rhodes knew. His own head started to throb. He'd thought it was getting better. Maybe he was just having sympathy pains, though why he should be sympathetic with the man who'd caused the wound, he wasn't sure.

"Is Dr. White certain about that?" he said. He could see

181

how mashing and striking would be different, but he felt as if he had to ask.

"He's certain. Besides, you can call the city and see what time the trash was picked up, but I'll bet it wasn't before seven o'clock Monday morning. And Dr. White says Kennedy'd been dead about twelve hours by that time."

Rhodes thanked Ballinger, took the report, and got out of there. He wondered if he could get a refund on those airplane tickets.

SEVENTEEN

Considering all the distractions that he'd had, it wasn't surprising that Rhodes didn't get around to cleaning the pistol until Thursday.

He'd taken it out of the car and left it in the office, but there had been quite a bit on his mind and he'd forgotten it. He was pretty sure that he was afflicted with a disease that Hack referred to as CRS—Can't Remember Stuff—something that had come on him about the same time that his eyes had started failing.

It wasn't that he forgot important things, just little ones. And the things he forgot were in his short-term memory. He still thought with pleasure of the accomplishments of baseball players like Ralph Kiner, Hank Sauer, or Johnny Mize; but though he still followed baseball closely every summer and read about the games of the Astros and Rangers in the paper each day, he couldn't recall the names of seven of the eight starters for either team.

Hack told him that this wasn't unusual.

"Hell," Hack said. "You're just gettin' old. You get my age, you won't even remember that you forgot somethin'."

Rhodes had been made amply aware in the last week

that growing older wasn't going to be any fun, and the memory bit was typical of the changes he was aware of in himself. He didn't like it much.

As soon as he found out from Ballinger about the cause of Kennedy's death, he had gone back to the jail and read Dr. White's report, which added little to the oral version he'd received from Ballinger.

Then he'd called the crime lab where he'd sent the grocery bag and asked for them to rush him the report. That had arrived Wednesday, but it was no help at all. A lot of grocery stores these days were switching to plastic bags; they had proved to be cheaper than paper and were convenient for small items, especially wet ones. The one that had been used on Lloyd Bobbit was a generic item, no advertising printed on it, and identical to those used in a number of stores in Blacklin County and the surrounding area. There were partial prints on the bag, but partials were not always accepted for the purpose of identification by the courts. Maybe if he could find a good match, they would help. Maybe not.

Rhodes was getting very worried. If Kennedy hadn't killed Bobbit, who had? And if Kennedy *had* killed Bobbit, who had killed Kennedy? And why? It was all more complicated than it had seemed, and Rhodes, who had thought the case was over now realized that he was right back where he had started, if not worse off.

He had at least been successful at one thing; he had kept the news of Kennedy's murder from leaking either to the news people, as represented by Red Rogers, or to Miss Bobbit. Everyone still believed the original story to be the true one and that Kennedy had died in an accident. That didn't help Rhodes with finding Kennedy's killer, but it did take some of the pressure off.

Not all the pressure. It was getting dangerously close to Saturday, and Rhodes had not canceled the airline tickets. It was going to be exceedingly difficult for him to leave the

184

county during a murder investigation, no matter how many vacation days he was owed, but he was going to have to do it. He couldn't disappoint Ivy.

And if they didn't go on the trip, she *would* be disappointed. She had found a bathing suit and some summer outfits, she had told her friends that she was going to Cozumel, and she had been studying a stack of travel brochures. Rhodes knew that there was no way out of the trip. He had to solve the crime.

But there didn't seem to be any clues. The grocery bag had been his best hope, and it had proved not to be useful.

He sifted through his suspects in Bobbit's death.

Mr. Patterson seemed the most unlikely, though money was always a powerful motive.

Miss Bobbit already had the money, and her father's death was an inconvenience. Rhodes thought she might have killed him simply to get rid of him. He was an embarrassment to her, standing out on the porch of the nursing home and announcing the theft of his teeth to all comers, and she was not the sort of person who enjoyed the kind of attention that called to her. Her main concern was to keep her name out of the newspapers, both when her father had disappeared and when he was killed. That seemed a farfetched motive, however.

Kennedy was the best suspect, even now. He obviously was a man with a violent temperament, if he had indeed killed Louis Horn in the argument at the dance. And Rhodes didn't think there was any question about that.

Bobbit had known of the long-ago murder, had even threatened to reveal the truth of the matter, according to old Mr. West, and that would have been enough to make Kennedy angry and perhaps frightened, maybe frightened enough to kill again. Besides, if Kennedy had not killed Bobbit, why had he run away from Sunny Dale?

Rhodes pondered those questions and others when he wasn't worrying about his impending marriage and honeymoon. To tell the truth, he was glad of the distraction the new perspective on the deaths gave him. Worrying about the murders kept his mind off the other things.

But pondering and worrying didn't get him anywhere. He went to the nursing home and talked to the Stuarts and to Mr. West, but he learned nothing new from them. He'd had the feeling earlier that Mr. West knew something that he wasn't telling, but the old man revealed nothing. If he did know anything, he was hiding it well. His more or less frozen face made it difficult to read anything in his expression.

Rhodes did remember to go by to get his stitches checked, get the results of his blood test, and to pick up the marriage license, but he almost forgot the last thing. Ivy reminded him again, however, and he got it done in between visits to the nursing home, worrying about the murders, and performing the normal chores of his office.

And so it wasn't until Thursday afternoon that Rhodes opened the bottom drawer of his desk and saw the pistol. He took it out and noticed something that he was surprised he had not noticed before.

The pistol had been fired. Twice.

It had been dark in the car, and Rhodes had hardly looked at the pistol. There was no reason he would have noticed it then.

When he had taken the gun in the jail and locked it in his desk, he had been in a hurry. There was too much going on, and Hack and Lawton had started in on him almost immediately with the story about the mooning.

He wished he had noticed the two missing rounds sooner, but it would not have made any difference to the outcome of the case. It would just have helped him to reach some conclusions earlier and taken some of the pressure off, because seeing the two empty chambers in the cylinder seemed to make everything click into place.

He put the pistol back in the desk, locked the drawer, and told Hack that he was going to visit Sunny Dale.

"You sure go out there a lot," Hack said. "You thinkin' about reservin' a room?"

Rhodes thought about his eyes and his failing memory. "Maybe I should," he said.

Hack laughed. "You got a few years on you yet. I bet you come back from Mexico feelin' like a colt again."

Rhodes hoped Hack was right, but he doubted it.

Mr. West's room was dark. The television set was quiet, and there was only a small lamp burning on the night stand.

Rhodes went on in anyway and sat in the chair beside the bed. Somehow, he didn't think that Mr. West was asleep.

He had been sitting in the chair for about five minutes when the old man spoke.

"What're you doing' here, Sheriff?" West said. "Visitin' the sick?"

"No," Rhodes said. "There's something that you and I have to discuss."

"What's that, Sheriff?"

"It's about Andy," Rhodes said. "Just how bad a job is he doing at the store?"

"Pretty bad," West admitted. "I told you that. He's not a businessman."

"I went by the courthouse and the bank today," Rhodes said. "You and Andy bought some land out there around the store and your house a couple of years ago, right before you had your stroke. Nearly five hundred acres. I guess you were thinking that fella was going to get the college restored a lot sooner than it looks like he will."

"Ha," West said. "Rate he's goin', it won't be done in another fifty years."

"It would have brought some business by the store if he'd gotten on with it, I guess."

"That's what we were thinkin'. Liven things up out that way, increase the value of the land. We were lookin' to make a little money."

"It doesn't look like a very good investment now, though," Rhodes said. "The restoration's going pretty slow, and Andy's missed a lot of payments on that land. Nearly all of them."

"We put up the store and the house as collateral," West said. "He's gonna lose 'em both. If I was there, it'd be different. I could always stir up the business."

Rhodes didn't know whether that was wishful thinking or the truth, but it didn't matter either way. "He's planning to marry Brenda Bobbit for her money, isn't he?"

West didn't respond. He just lay there, his head twisted to the side.

"But he was afraid that Bobbit might be a little crazy. He was pretty senile, for sure. Maybe he wouldn't let Brenda use the money the way she wanted to, wouldn't let her give it to her husband."

"I don't know what you're gettin' at," West said.

"Andy didn't know Brenda had her father's power of attorney. She already had control of the money, but he didn't know that. So he thought he ought to get rid of Mr. Bobbit just to make sure he wouldn't cause any trouble."

"You don't know what you're talkin' about," West said.

"I think I do," Rhodes said. "Andy came out here, probably sat right where I'm sitting. You say you were taking a nap that day. Maybe you were. Maybe you didn't know that your son got up and went into Bobbit's room, tied him to the bed, and slipped that bag over his head. Maybe you did know."

"He . . . he didn't do that," West said.

"I think he did," Rhodes said. "I think that Maurice

Kennedy saw him coming out of the room, too. I don't quite know what happened then, but I think Andy saw Kennedy and Kennedy knew it. When he found out that Bobbit was dead, he got out of here, either because he thought he'd be blamed or because he was afraid of Andy."

"You're just . . . guessing," West, said. "You don't know any of that."

He was right, at least partly. Rhodes wasn't sure about everything. It was possible that Kennedy hadn't seen West coming out of the room. Kennedy might just have found the body, figured that he would be blamed, and run away. But Rhodes was sure Andy West would have tried to get rid of Kennedy sooner or later, to shift suspicion away from himself. And that was why Kennedy had to get West first.

"I think Kennedy went out to Andy's house Sunday night," Rhodes went on. "He'd been hiding out, and he was tired of it, so he was going to get rid of Andy. He got rid of Louis Horn, and he thought he could handle your son. He fired two shots at him, but he missed. Andy went after him. Kennedy was on foot, but maybe he got away. I think he managed to get part of the way back to town, but Andy caught up with him and killed him. Hit him in the head and put him in a dumpster. That was a good move. It was only an accident that we found Kennedy's body."

West lay quietly in the bed. Rhodes waited for him to say something, but the old man was apparently not going to speak.

"Did you know any of this?" Rhodes said after a few minutes had passed.

"I don't even know it now," West said. "You don't, either. You can't prove a thing except that we owe a little money."

"A lot of money," Rhodes said. "The bank is going to foreclose this month."

"Don't matter. You can't make me say anything about my son. I don't know a thing. You better go on out of here, Sheriff. I feel like I need a nap." West closed his eyes.

Rhodes sat in the chair for a few more minutes, then got up. He had hoped that Mr. West would tell him something, because the old man was right. Rhodes had no proof of what he was saying. He was sure he was right, however, on most of the points. He did know that the bag *could* have come from West's store, but he couldn't prove that it had. He wasn't especially hopeful about the partial prints.

There was always the chance that when West had caught up with Kennedy and killed him, the body had been put in West's old Ford, however. If that had happened, there might be some evidence remaining to prove an association between West and Kennedy. Fibers, blood, something.

It would certainly have been easier if Mr. West had told Rhodes that his son had killed Bobbit. Now there was nothing to do except confront Andy and see if he would be any more helpful.

It was getting late when Rhodes drove out to the Obert Road. The weather had not gotten any warmer, though the wind had stopped blowing a couple of days before. There was a thorough chill in the air, and Rhodes was sure the temperature would drop down below freezing again that night.

He turned on the lights of the county car before he got to West's store, and they reflected off the body of an old gray Pontiac as he pulled into the drive. It was almost a surprise to see that West actually had a customer. There was another car parked by the side of the building as well. Business was booming.

Rhodes stopped the car and got out. It was nearly dark, and he felt the cold invade his clothing immediately. The fluorescent light from inside the store came through the windows and made rectangles on the ground.

Rhodes went inside, announced by the cow bell on the

door. West was handing a plastic bag to a man and a woman whom Rhodes vaguely recognized. He knew they must live in the area. They were bundled up in heavy coats. Rhodes looked around for whoever was in the second car, but he didn't see anyone.

"Thank you now," West said to his customers with a hearty false cheerfulness. "Y'all come back."

The man mumbled something, and he and the woman turned to go. There wasn't much in the sack. Rhodes thought they had probably stopped in because they had forgotten to buy something essential, like bologna or Dr Pepper, in town. He spoke to them as they brushed past him, and then they were out the door like ghosts, not even jangling the bell.

"What can I do for you, Sheriff?" West said when they were gone.

Rhodes heard car doors slam outside, heard the old Pontiac labor into life, valves clattering.

"Sounds like they could use a tune-up," West said.

"Maybe so," Rhodes said. "I want to talk to you about something else, though. About Lloyd Bobbit and Maurice Kennedy."

"What about 'em?" West said. "I thought all that was settled."

"So did everybody else. That was before I found out Kennedy didn't die in the trash truck."

"So what? He's dead anyway."

"Yes," Rhodes agreed. "And I think you killed him. Bobbit, too."

West smiled. "You been smokin' some of that dope evidence down at the jail, Sheriff?"

"I should have known when you said that Miss Bobbit hadn't told you about the power of attorney," Rhodes said. "Why should that have made a difference to you? Now I know. You need the money. Right now. Either that, or you lose everything."

"So what?" West said again. "That doesn't mean a thing as far as those old men are concerned.

"I think it does. I think you were marrying Miss Bobbit for her money. I think you were upset when you found out she had the power of attorney and that it ended with her father's death. You'd killed two men for no reason; in fact, you'd made things worse for yourself."

Someone stepped out of the shadows at the rear of the store. There was a doorway back there that led to a little added-on room where West stored a small supply of feed and grain.

"Did you do that?" Miss Bobbit said, coming out into the light from where she had been listening. "Did you kill my father?"

"Hell, no. Why would I do that?" West said. He turned and started toward her.

"Are you marrying me for my money?" she said. Her voice had taken on a tinge of emotion that Rhodes had never heard in it before. She wasn't quite the cold fish that she had seemed. It just took more than murder to affect her; it took something like the realization that she was being used by someone like West.

She was standing behind the refrigerated meat cooler when West got to her. "Don't listen to him," West said. "He doesn't know what he's talking about."

"You were awfully upset about that power of attorney," she said. "After the sheriff left, you yelled at me."

"I'm sorry about that," West said. "I didn't mean to."

"I know I'm not very attractive," she said. "I know that. But I've got a good name. You're not going to take that away from me."

"He doesn't know what he's talking about," West said, looking over his shoulder at Rhodes. "He's just trying to cause trouble. You know he's wrong."

"I don't think so," Miss Bobbit said. West looked back at her. "I think he's right. You were mean to me about the power of attorney. And you *did* get me to say I'd make the payment to the bank for you."

"Shut up about the payment," West said.

"When I told you that my father had been killed, you weren't even surprised," she said. "You were there that afternoon, too. Weren't you?"

"What if I was? I didn't kill him." There was an undertone of whining in West's tone now.

"I think you did," Rhodes said, deciding it was time he got back in the conversation. "The bag on Mr. Bobbit's head was identical to the one you just handed that man and woman. And there were fingerprints on it." That wasn't stretching the truth any more than he had stretched the definition of "planning" to Ivy and Hack. "I think we'll find a good match with yours when we check them."

"Goddamn it," West said to Miss Bobbit. "This is all your fault."

He put out his right hand and reached for something that Rhodes couldn't see while grabbing Miss Bobbit's wrist with his left. He pulled her to him quickly, bending her arm behind her back and turning her around. He stepped out from behind the cooler, shoving her in front of him. He had a meat cleaver in his right hand.

"There might even be some human blood on the blunt side of that cleaver," Rhodes said. "Maurice Kennedy's blood. It's hard to remove it completely."

"You're pretty damn smart, aren't you, Sheriff," West said.

"Not very," Rhodes said, reaching for his gun.

"Don't do that." West brandished the cleaver. "This thing's plenty sharp. I can cut her head off before you know it."

"You wouldn't dare," Miss Bobbit said.

"The hell I wouldn't." He spoke in Miss Bobbit's ear. "Let's go get in that nice car of yours and take us a little ride." West walked toward the door, keeping Miss Bobbit in front.

When they got near Rhodes, she made a quick movement, trying to break away, but West snapped her back to him, twisting her wrist sharply. She yelped at the pain in her arm.

"Just step back, Sheriff," West said. "You let us by, you hear?"

Rhodes stepped back, keeping his eyes on West and Miss Bobbit. They went through the door, the cow bell clanging.

Rhodes went after them.

He hadn't gotten outside when West started yelling, so he didn't know what Miss Bobbit had done to him. Whatever it was, it must have been painful. By the time Rhodes got out the door, Miss Bobbit was running toward the back of the store. West was in hot pursuit, holding the cleaver at shoulder level and yelling for her to stop.

Rhodes pulled his pistol and watched them run. If he had been the world's best marksman, he might have risked a shot, but as it was he didn't want to try. It was dark, the moon hidden in the clouds, and he was just as likely to hit Miss Bobbit as West.

He didn't know where Miss Bobbit was headed. Probably she was just running, trying to get away from West. There wasn't much in back of the store except an open field and Obert's Hill behind her. West's house was back there, too, but Miss Bobbit wasn't headed for it. She was going for the hill.

Rhodes had sometimes thought that Obert's Hill would have made an ideal location for the B Westerns of his childhood. He would not have been surprised, in those days, to see Randolph Scott or Allan "Rocky" Lane riding down the side of the hill, weaving in and out among the oak trees and the big rocks.

Just over the crest of the hill were the college buildings and what was left of the town. The buildings would have spoiled the illusion, but they couldn't be seen from where Rhodes was now.

It appeared that Miss Bobbit was going to climb the hill if West didn't catch her first. Rhodes holstered his pistol and started after them. He didn't know what else to do.

He wasn't good at running, even at the best of times. Not enough work on the exercise bike, he told himself, and too many bruises. His chest and back still hurt, and running wasn't doing them any good. Every step seemed to jar his head, too.

It wasn't like they were running on level ground, either. This was uncultivated land, with rocks, holes, fire ant mounds, sticks, dead grass, live weeds. Rhodes hoped he didn't break an ankle.

Miss Bobbit was making good time. Rhodes was surprised that she was so fast. Maybe she would get away and he would catch up with West.

He hoped that he would still be able to breathe if he did.

C H A P T E R

EIGHTEEN

Miss Bobbit had a good lead, but she didn't have good luck. She fell down.

It wasn't really her fault. Rhodes saw something spring up practically out of the ground in front of her and barrel across the field like a bowling ball gone berserk.

Rhodes thought it was probably an armadillo. They were sort of round and low to the ground, and despite their very short, stubby legs they could travel a lot faster than a man. Or a bowling ball.

It scared Miss Bobbit, jumping up out of the dark like that, not that Rhodes blamed her. It would have scared him, too, if it had popped up right in front of him while West was chasing him through the night with a cleaver, looking like a character from a teen-age splatter movie. West was already wearing the white store apron with a few splashes of blood on it. All he needed was a hockey mask. It would have been funny if it hadn't been so serious.

Miss Bobbit let out a little scream, tried to reverse her field, got her foot caught somehow, and fell forward into a stand of dead milkweeds.

Rhodes had a clear shot at West now, but he had run

nearly fifty yards. Squeezing off a shot after he'd run that far, he would be about as likely to hit West as he would be to hit a nailhead. He kept running.

West reached Miss Bobbit. He bent down and dragged her to her feet. Miss Bobbit was twisting, spitting, kicking, and trying to bite.

West drew back the cleaver to hit her just as Rhodes crashed into them.

They all three went down in a pile. Rhodes didn't know how the others felt, but he was pretty sure they weren't hurting as much as he was.

He tried to get his hands on West's arm, the one with the cleaver, but West wasn't cooperating. He rolled over and swung at Rhodes's head.

Rhodes moved aside, but the edge caught him a glancing blow over his right eye, laying back the skin. Rhodes had dragged the back of his head across the rough ground, and he felt the wound back there opening up, too.

Miss Bobbit landed on West's back, clawing at his eyes, before he could swing again. He tried to shake her off, but he was on the ground and couldn't get any leverage.

Rhodes got to his knees and got his pistol out, but by then West had managed to get part-way up. Miss Bobbit was still writhing on his back, and he heaved her over his shoulder at Rhodes.

She crashed into Rhodes, and they fell heavily. Rhodes lost his grip on the pistol.

Not again, he thought.

West was standing now. He pulled Miss Bobbit off Rhodes and threw her aside. He wasn't interested in her anymore. He wanted Rhodes.

Rhodes saw the cleaver coming out of the dark and twisted his head. The cleaver thudded into the ground. West jerked it out and got ready to try again, but Rhodes kicked him in the knee.

Rhodes didn't quite hit it straight on, so the knee didn't

198

break, but it made a satisfactory cracking noise. West stumbled back and Rhodes got to his feet. He knew the pistol was there somewhere, but he didn't see it. He felt blood dripping down past one eye. More stitches. If he lived to go on his honeymoon, he was going to look like he'd been assembled by Dr. Frankenstein.

He saw West staggering around and went after him. Miss Bobbit was going after him, too, but West didn't panic. He clipped her on the chin, and she went down. Then he singled out Rhodes again, and this time he tried something different.

He threw the cleaver.

It hit Rhodes squarely in the middle of his chest.

If the sharp edge had struck him there, it would have split him open like a ripe cantaloupe, but it was the blunt end, the end opposite the handle, that hit him.

Not that it didn't hurt. It hurt like hell, and Rhodes let out a yell. West was strong, and Rhodes was already severely bruised. This time there were going to be cracked ribs for sure.

Rhodes stumbled backward and sat down hard, right on a fire ant mound.

The ants swarmed out, instantly maddened to a stinging frenzy, as was the way with fire ants. They clung to Rhodes's pants and shirt, but that wasn't so bad. It was the ones on his hands that hurt.

He brushed them off as fast as he could. West was coming for him, hobbling on his injured knee.

Miss Bobbit was back up again. She was tougher than she looked. She got in between Rhodes and West and grabbed West's arms. She slowed him down, but she didn't stop him. He knocked her aside and kept on coming.

Rhodes couldn't stop him either. He might have been able to do so under normal conditions, but these weren't normal conditions. He had a cracked rib or two, fire ants crawling all over him and stinging his hands, and blood from the cut over his eye was dripping down his face.

West lowered his head and slammed into Rhodes's midsection, knocking the air out of the sheriff and pushing him back down. They landed a few feet away from the fire ants, which was the only good thing about the situation.

Rhodes managed to make a fist and hit West in the side of the head twice. Then he grabbed West's right ear and started twisting. He was hoping to tear it off West's head, or at least make West think that was going to happen, but West didn't even seem to mind. He had succeeded in working himself into such a state of anger that nothing reached him. The message about the pain in his ear wasn't getting through to his brain.

Rhodes, on the other hand, was getting a definite message, and the message was that he wasn't going to be able to keep on breathing for much longer. West had his thick fingers wrapped around Rhodes's throat and was squeezing as hard as he could.

His thumbs were crushing Rhodes's windpipe, and Rhodes thought that those thumbs were probably going to meet West's fingers, which were on the back of Rhodes's neck, in a very short time.

But by then, Rhodes would be past caring.

In fact, he was almost past caring now. He could feel West's hot breath on his face and he could see West's madly staring eyes. Beyond West's head was the blackness of the sky, or maybe it was some other kind of blackness, because after a minute, the blackness was all that Rhodes could see, and after that he couldn't see anything at all.

The next thing he heard was Ruth Grady's voice. He hadn't expected to hear her. He hadn't expected to hear anything ever again.

200

She said, "Where's Sheriff Rhodes?" Her voice was faint, and she sounded very far away.

"Over here somewhere," Miss Bobbit said. "With Andy."

Rhodes gradually became aware of a heavy weight on his chest, pinning him to the ground. That was probably Andy, all right.

Rhodes was very cold, and he felt something wet soaking through his jacket and into his shirt.

Blood? If it was, he didn't know for sure whether it was his own or Andy's. His throat felt like someone had stuck a hot poker down it, but he didn't remember bleeding.

Then he thought of the cut over his eye. Could that be it?

He opened his eyes. He still couldn't see much. It was too dark, but he thought he could see a flashlight beam not far away. He closed his eyes again. He was too tired to keep them open.

"There they are," Miss Bobbit said.

"Oh my God," Ruth said. "Are they both dead?"

"I don't know," Miss Bobbit said. "They might be. I couldn't figure out how to shoot the gun at first."

She must have found his pistol and shot West, then called the jail, Rhodes guessed. He was glad his mind was working enough to figure things out, even if they were only simple things.

The flashlight was on him now. He kept his eyes closed and tried to say that he was fine, but the sound that came out was like a rusty gate swinging open.

Miss Bobbit stifled a scream, but Ruth didn't waste any time. She pulled Andy West off Rhodes and shoved the body aside. It fell to the ground like a sack of seed corn. Ruth knelt down on one knee.

"Can you hear me, Sheriff?" she said.

Rhodes decided not to try talking again. He just nodded. That hurt even more than talking, however. He opened his eyes.

"The ambulance will be here in a minute," Ruth said. "Do you want to sit up?"

"No," Rhodes croaked. Then he heard the siren, and in a minute or so he could see the lights of the ambulance bouncing across the field.

When the ambulance got there, the attendants loaded Rhodes in the back as tenderly as they could and then stuck West in with him. They rode back to town together, but no one was going to be able to do much for West. Miss Bobbit had shot him in the back five times.

Rhodes did not have a good night.

Ruth had called Ivy, who met them at the hospital emergency room as they were taking Rhodes inside. She walked beside the gurney.

Rhodes didn't want to look at her. It would have been much easier to keep his eyes closed and pretend that he had passed out, but he was supposed to be the sheriff. The sheriff couldn't be a coward. He'd faced West's cleaver. He could face Ivy.

She looked relieved to see that he was alive, but she was not happy with him. "You must think you're John Wayne," she said.

"No," Rhodes growled. "Foghorn Winslow."

That got a smile. Ivy remembered Foghorn Winslow. Then she said, "What's the matter with your voice?"

Rhodes didn't say anything. One of the attendants pointed to Rhodes's throat. Rhodes heard Ivy suck in her breath. He figured his throat didn't look too good.

It took the E.R. doctor a while to take care of Rhodes. It bothered Rhodes that the doctor looked like a high school student. One of the real problems with getting older was that you had to trust all your ailments and contusions to people who looked hardly old enough to have a driver's license.

Rhodes had to get the back of his head restitched, and he needed eight more stitches over his eye. The doctor's touch was deft, even if he did look like a fugitive from a Clearasil ad.

Then there were the ribs. Two of them were slightly cracked.

The good news was that they wouldn't have to be taped; the bad news was that they were going to be very painful.

"For a month, at least," the doctor said cheerfully. "Any movement at all is likely to cause a sharp pain. Planning on doing any moving around for a while?"

"I, ah, I'm getting married tomorrow," Rhodes rasped.

"Well, well, well," the doctor said. He smiled. "Well, well, well."

Rhodes sneaked a look at Ivy. Her shoulders shook as she laughed silently. Rhodes didn't see anything funny about it himself.

"We'll be keeping you overnight for observation," the doctor said. "What time is the wedding?"

"Eleven o'clock," Ivy said.

"We can let him go by then," the doctor said. "If he can walk."

"He'll walk," Ivy said. "Even if I have to carry him."

Later, in Rhodes's room, she was not quite so chipper.

"One of these days," she said, "you're going to get into a terrible mess like that one tonight, and you aren't going to walk away from it."

"I didn't exactly walk away from this one," Rhodes said. His voice was a little better, but his throat still felt as if he'd swallowed a cactus. He had sucked a lemon, which he didn't think helped much, and gargled something the doctor had prescribed.

"I *could* have walked, though," he said. Then he added, "I think."

Ivy sighed and looked at him with a frown. "I'm never going to get used to it," she said. "You haven't ever thought about changing careers, I don't suppose?"

Rhodes knew that she didn't really mean it, but he said, "Change to what? I don't know how to do anything else."

"I guess I'll just have to put up with it, then," Ivy said, but she was still frowning. "Do you want me to go by and feed Speedo tonight?"

Rhodes said that he did. "He's practically your dog, too. As of tomorrow, he'll be community property."

"Not exactly. You had him before we got married."

"What's mine is yours," Rhodes said.

Ivy finally smiled. "And don't you forget it," she said.

Rhodes didn't want to take anything to make him sleep, but the nurse insisted. Since he didn't know which pills were for the pain—and he *did* want those—and which ones were for sleeping, he didn't argue much; but sleeping pills always made him dream.

Tonight was no exception.

He dreamed again and again that Andy West was sitting on his chest, choking the life out of him. And in every dream, Rhodes seemed to see Miss Bobbit standing behind West, pointing a pistol at her fiancé's back.

"What are you waiting for?" Rhodes wanted to yell at her, but he couldn't because West had that death grip on his throat.

Miss Bobbit just stood there, watching.

Then, just as Rhodes was about to wake up, Miss Bobbit would fire the pistol. Oddly enough, instead of waking Rhodes, the sound of the shots would always put him back to sleep.

He woke up the next morning at seven fifty-eight by his watch. His head felt as if it were stuffed with cotton, another reason he didn't like the sleeping pills.

He forced himself to sit up, ignoring the pain that shot through him from just about every part of his body. Even his legs were sore. They hadn't been injured; he just wasn't used to running.

He got dressed, called the nurse, and checked himself out. He didn't feel like driving. He felt even older than Lloyd Bobbit had been, and he phoned Ruth to come after him. His voice was almost back to normal, but his throat still hurt.

While he waited, he thought about the dream and wondered what it had meant. Probably nothing. Then he thought about something that West had said. He asked if he could use the hospital phone again, and this time he called Tom Dunstable.

It was early, but Dunstable was in his office. He said that he would be glad to talk to Rhodes.

Ruth took him by his house first. He fed the dog and got the wedding ring he had bought a month before. It was nothing fancy, just a simple gold band.

Ruth then drove him to the lawyer's office and he struggled out of the car and hobbled inside. An old song kept running through his head. "Hand Me Down My Walking Cane."

"Godamighty," Dunstable said, looking up as Rhodes entered. "You'll excuse me if I don't get up. What the devil happened to you?"

Rhodes told him, just hitting the high points.

"Well, I hate to say it, but you look a little the worse for wear. Weren't you supposed to be getting married here pretty soon?"

"This morning," Rhodes said. "Eleven o'clock."

"Godamighty," Dunstable said again, shaking his head. "Well, I guess you didn't come here to talk about a personal injury suit, seeing how as the guy who injured you is dead. What can I do for you?"

Rhodes asked him the question that had been bothering him. Dunstable's answer was about what he had expected.

"You sure you don't want me to come in?" Ruth Grady said. They were parked outside Miss Bobbit's house.

"I'll take care of it," Rhodes said. He hadn't told her why they were there. Getting out of the car wasn't any easier this time than it had been before.

Miss Bobbit answered the door. She had on different glasses this morning. Rhodes wondered if she had lost the others in the fighting. His own had disappeared from his shirt pocket, and he was planning to buy another pair.

"What is it, Sheriff?" Miss Bobbit said.

"I just wanted to talk to you for a minute," Rhodes said. "And thank you for saving my life last night."

"Come in, then," Miss Bobbit said.

He followed her into the living room. When she turned to face him, he said, "You knew all along, didn't you?"

"Knew what?" She was the cold fish again.

"Knew a lot of things. You knew that the power of attorney automatically ended with your father's death, for one."

She started to say something, but Rhodes didn't let her. "Don't bother to lie about it. I talked to Tom Dunstable this morning. He arranged it, and he told me that he explained everything to you, particularly that part. I don't know why I would have ever thought otherwise. You knew, but you didn't tell West. I wonder why?"

"You probably think you already know."

"I do. I think you wanted him to kill your father. It was an easy way to get rid of him, and you could shift the blame to Maurice Kennedy simply enough. It worked out very well."

Miss Bobbit smiled tightly. "I don't know what you're talking about."

"Sure you do," Rhodes said. He wasn't smiling. "If West was caught in the act, that was too bad, but there was every chance he'd get away with it. He thought he was putting one over on you, but he knew whose fault it was. It dawned on him last night."

Rhodes was sure now that the emotion he had heard in Miss Bobbit's voice in West's store was not the result of her discovering that she had been used by West; it was fear of West's realizing that he was the one being used all along.

"I don't know what kind of hints you dropped," Rhodes continued, "but I'm sure West picked up on them. He was sure that with your father out of the way he'd get the money, and you were glad to be free of an old man who was causing you embarrassment."

"I could sue you for slander," Miss Bobbit said.

"You could," Rhodes said. "But you won't. I don't think you want anyone else in Clearview to hear all this, much less get it discussed in open court."

"You could never prove it. You'd look like a fool."

"Probably," Rhodes said. "I'm not going to try proving it."

"You're not? Then why are you here?" She seemed genuinely curious.

"I told you. I wanted to thank you for saving me. Even if you were doing it to shut West up." Rhodes paused. "There's just one other thing."

"And what's that?"

"I was wondering why you waited so long to shoot him," Rhodes said.

"I don't know much about guns. I couldn't figure out how to use it after I stumbled across it," Miss Bobbit said.

"You point it and pull the trigger," Rhodes said.

"Well, I—"

"You wanted me out of the way, too," Rhodes said. "It occurred to you that I might have figured it out. There was no way I could prosecute you, but you couldn't stand the idea that I might know. You should have waited just a little longer."

"I couldn't," Miss Bobbit said. Her voice was calm and steady. "Andy was through with you. He looked around at me and yelled something at me. I couldn't even understand what he was saying, but I knew that I couldn't wait any longer."

"Too bad," Rhodes said.

"What are you going to do?"

"Not a thing. There's no doubt you killed West in self-defense. If I filed charges against you on that, they'd never clear the grand jury. And there's no way I can prove you manipulated West into killing your father. Even he didn't know until it was too late."

"I'm not admitting that I did that. I *didn't* do it."

"Yes," Rhodes said. "You did."

"Let me ask you once more. What are you going to do?"

"I'll give you the same answer. Not a thing."

"Then why did you come here? It certainly wasn't to thank me."

"No, it wasn't. Not really. I just came to tell you that I know what you did. You can go on being a respected member of the community, thinking about your good name if you want to, pretending to be the devoted daughter, but *I know*."

Miss Bobbit looked at him stonily. "You'd better leave now," she said.

Rhodes turned and shuffled out of the room and let himself out of the house. Before he shut the door behind him, he looked back. Miss Bobbit stood exactly where he had left her, her back rigid, her eyes staring straight ahead.

The door didn't make a sound when it closed.

"Is everything all right?" Ruth said when Rhodes eased himself back into the car.

"Everything's fine," Rhodes said. "I just wanted to thank her for saving me. What time is it?"

"Ten forty-five," Ruth said.

"I guess we'd better get on over to the courthouse, then, hadn't we?"

"I guess we had," Ruth agreed.

CHAPTER

NINETEEN

No place in Clearview was very far from any other place. They got to the courthouse in plenty of time.
Rhodes was surprised to see that the judge's chambers were crowded when he and Ruth entered. Hack was there, along with Mrs. McGee.

"Lawton wanted to come, too," Hack said. "But somebody had to stay there with those engineers, so we flipped a coin. I won."

"What about the engineers?" Rhodes said.

"You don't have to worry about them. They're doin' whatever it is they do, lookin' and tappin' and all that. Lawton's got everything under control."

Rhodes hoped so.

James Allen and Mrs. Wilkie were there, too. Allen grinned and shook Rhodes's hand. "Good work on that murder case, Sheriff," he said. "You're making the county look good in law enforcement circles. I stopped by the jail to check on the engineers. Everything's going along just fine."

"That's what Hack says," Rhodes told him. "What about the lawsuit?"

"I'm still betting that the lawyer's going to ask for a settlement from the county, and nothing at all from you boys over at the jail. You can keep your million dollars."

"Ivy will be glad to hear it," Rhodes said.

Mrs. Wilkie just stood there and didn't say anything. She looked like she might be going to cry, and Rhodes hoped that she wouldn't.

Rhodes was surprised to see that Mr. Patterson was there, along with Mr. and Mrs. Stuart.

"Wouldn't have missed it," Mr. Stuart said. "I told my wife, they came to our weddin', and we're gonna be at theirs."

"That's right," Mrs. Stuart said. "And here we are." She was standing in her walker, and Rhodes wondered how on earth she had gotten up the stairs. He had barely made it up the stairs himself; there was no question that the court house needed an elevator, and the sooner the better.

Kathy was there, too. There was a young man with her. "Good Lord, Daddy," Kathy said. "What happened?"

Rhodes looked around the room for help, but everyone studiously avoided his eyes. Judge Parry was looking at the unlighted cigar in his hand, Hack was talking to Mrs. McGee, Allen was congratulating Ruth on her part in solving the murders, and Mrs. Wilkie was looking out the window.

"I, uh, got into a little scrape," Rhodes said.

"A *little* scrape! I wonder if I'm going to have to move back home and take care of you."

Hack decided to come to Rhodes's rescue. "Your daddy's a hero," he said. "Solved three murders, one of 'em that happened sixty years or so back. Ever'body was fooled about what was goin' on, but not the sheriff."

"Dead heroes don't do anyone any good," Kathy said. "Where's Ivy? I think I ought to have a talk with her."

"Uh, don't you want to introduce me to this young man that's standing here?" Rhodes said.

212

"Oh," Kathy said. "Dad, this is Greg Pollack. Greg, this is my father, Dan Rhodes."

Rhodes liked Pollack's looks. He wasn't big, but he was solid, with a strong chin and thick black hair, cut short like a lot of men's these days, with no sideburns at all. He had brown eyes that looked right at you and a dimple in his right cheek when he smiled, which he did when he and Rhodes shook hands.

"Glad to meet you, Sheriff," Pollack said. "Kathy's told me a lot about you. She didn't say anything about you getting into a lot of scrapes, though."

"I don't like to think about it," Kathy said. She reminded Rhodes of her mother, and never more so than when she was trying to take care of him. He wondered why everyone wanted to do that.

"Ivy and I are going to Cozumel," Rhodes said.

"You're changing the subject," Kathy said. "But I'm glad you're going. You need a vacation. The salt water's going to sting those cuts, I'm afraid."

"Maybe I'll just sit on the beach and soak up the sun," Rhodes said. "Where's Ivy?"

"She'll be here in just a minute," Hack said. "You're not supposed to see the bride before the wedding starts."

"Speaking of getting started," Parry said. "I think it's about time. Ruth, why don't you step down the hall and bring in the future Mrs. Rhodes."

Ruth left the room. Rhodes felt his throat getting tight. It was probably just a result of the choking West had given him. He wondered why the room was so warm. The county could cut back on the heating and save a lot of money.

"Sheriff, you come on over here," Parry said, motioning Rhodes toward his desk.

Rhodes walked over to Parry.

"Who's the best man?" Parry said.

"That would be Hack," Rhodes said. Hack walked over and joined them, just as Ruth and Ivy came into the room.

Ivy was wearing a gray suit with a white blouse and carrying a small bouquet of white carnations. Rhodes wondered who had bought it for her. She was smiling broadly, and Rhodes felt a tingling sensation in his toes. He also felt his throat getting tighter.

Hack was humming "The Wedding March," very quietly and slightly off-key.

Everyone cleared out of Ivy's way as she started toward the desk. Kathy walked just in front of her.

When they got to the desk, Kathy stepped aside and Ivy stopped beside Rhodes. She put out a hand and took his arm as they faced Parry.

"Well, now," Parry said. "Is there anyone here who's going to voice any objections to my joining this couple in matrimony?"

Rhodes thought about Mrs. Wilkie. He held his breath, but no one said anything.

"I guess we'd better get started, then," Parry said. "Do you have a ring, Sheriff?"

Rhodes reached in his pocket and brought out the ring. He thought he heard a sigh of relief from somewhere, but he didn't look to see where.

"Good," Parry said, and in less time than Rhodes would have thought possible, he and Ivy were being pronounced man and wife.

"You can kiss the bride," Parry said.

Rhodes had worried about that part. He'd thought he might be too embarrassed, especially in front of a crowd.

But it turned out that he wasn't, after all.